DORLING KINDERSLEY *CLASSICS*

ROBIN HOOD

Dorling Kindersley
LONDON, NEW YORK, SYDNEY, DELHI,
PARIS, MUNICH and JOHANNESBURG

A RETELLING BASED ON THE ORIGINAL MEDIEVAL BALLADS

Editor Nicholas Turpin
Art Editor Ian Campbell
Senior Editor Marie Greenwood
Series Art Editor Jane Thomas
Production Katy Holmes, Louise Barratt
Managing Art Editor Chris Fraser
Picture Research Louise Thomas and Elizabeth Bacon
DTP Designer Kim Browne

For Emily Cross

Published in the United States by Dorling Kindersley Publishing, Inc.
375 Hudson Street, New York, New York, 10014
First American Edition, 1997
Paperback edition published in 2000
4 6 8 10 9 7 5 3

Library of Congress Cataloging-in-Publication Data
Philip, Neal.
Robin Hood/adapted by Neil Philip; illustrated by Nick Harris -- 1st American ed.
p. cm. --(Dorling Kindersley read and listen)
Includes an audio tape featuring a reading of the text with special effects and music.
Summary: Recounts the life and adventures of Robin Hood, who, with his band of followers, lived in Sherwood Forest as an outlaw dedicated to fighting tyranny.
Illustrated notes throughout the text explain the historical background of the story.
ISBN 0-7894-5462-9 (pb & tape)
1. Robin Hood (Legendary character)--Legends. [1. Robin Hood (Legendary character)--Legends. 2. Folklore--England.] I. Harris, Neil, ill. II. Title. III. Series.
PZ8.1.P55 Ro 2000
398.2'0942'02--dc21
99-050013

Color reproduction by Bright Arts
Printed by L.Rex in China

for our complete
catalog visit
www.dk.com

DORLING KINDERSLEY *CLASSICS*

ROBIN HOOD

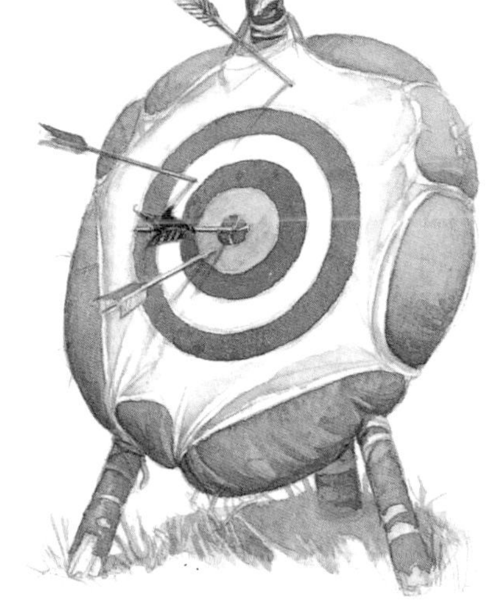

NEIL PHILIP

Illustrated by NICK HARRIS

A Dorling Kindersley Book

CONTENTS

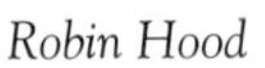

Robin Hood

Marian Fitzwalter

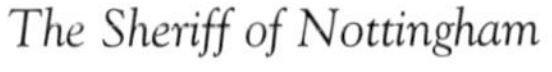

The Sheriff of Nottingham

Sir Guy of Gisborne

Little John

Friar Tuck

Will Scarlet

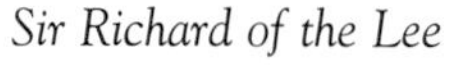

Sir Richard of the Lee

Lord Fitzwalter

King Richard

INTRODUCTION

Who was Robin Hood?
Everyone has heard of the outlaw who lived in Sherwood Forest, in England. But the stories of Robin Hood are legend, not history. They may have been based on the exploits of a real outlaw, such as the "Robert Hood, fugitive" who is listed in the records of the English courts of 1225. But no one knows for certain who Robin Hood was, or if he even existed.

In the 14th century, ballads (songs that tell stories) about Robin became well known. This version is based on the earliest ballads, but includes much that was added as Robin's fame grew. By the late 15th century, Robin featured as a character in games that were played in May to mark the beginning of summer. Marian and a friar also appeared in the games, and so probably became linked with Robin – Marian as his sweetheart and the friar as Friar Tuck. By 1600, Robin had become associated (in plays) with Robert, Earl of Huntingdon, who lived during the reign of Richard I (1189–99). Stories of Robin Hood survive because outlaws and rebels are attractive characters, especially those who rob not for gain, but in the cause of justice for common people. The special quality of this *Eyewitness Classic* is to bring Robin's medieval world to life. We see photographs and pictures of kings, peasants, merchants, and noblemen. We see the outlaws and their weapons, and the trees and animals of the forest in which they live. As we read, we can picture joining Robin and his men in the freedom of the greenwood.

Neil Philip

Robin Hood and his Merry Men in Sherwood Forest, Warren Edmund George (1834–1909)

ROBIN'S COUNTRY

In this book, Robin Hood's enemy is the sheriff of Nottingham and his home is Sherwood Forest, north of Nottingham. These are real places – although the forest has shrunk and Nottingham has grown since Robin's day.

Historically, Robin can be traced to many places. A manuscript of c.1400–25 in Lincoln Cathedral declares, "Robin Hood in Sherwood stood." But other references around the same date place him in the forest of Barnsdale, in South Yorkshire. There is no firm evidence to settle the question. We may still wander through Sherwood Forest, or see the gatehouse of Nottingham's medieval castle. But there is nothing that allows us to say with absolute confidence, "Robin Hood was here."

Whatever the reality, Robin Hood's story is the same. The outlaw is in the forest and the sheriff, his enemy, is in the town. The contrast is between civilization and wilderness, between imprisonment and freedom. Wherever we build walls, the wild greenwood is beyond them, and in it Robin's spirit still lives.

Nottingham
Huntingdon
London

The action of this story takes place in northern and central England.

Rolling green hills covered large areas of England in medieval times.

Sir Richard of the Lee was from Lee, a village in the valley of Wyresdale.

The village of Gisborne (now spelled Gisburn) was home to Sir Guy of Gisborne, b he spent most of his tim with the sheriff.

Kirklees Priory is now a ruin, but was once a home to nuns.

Deer roamed throughout the dense, wild woodland of medieval England.

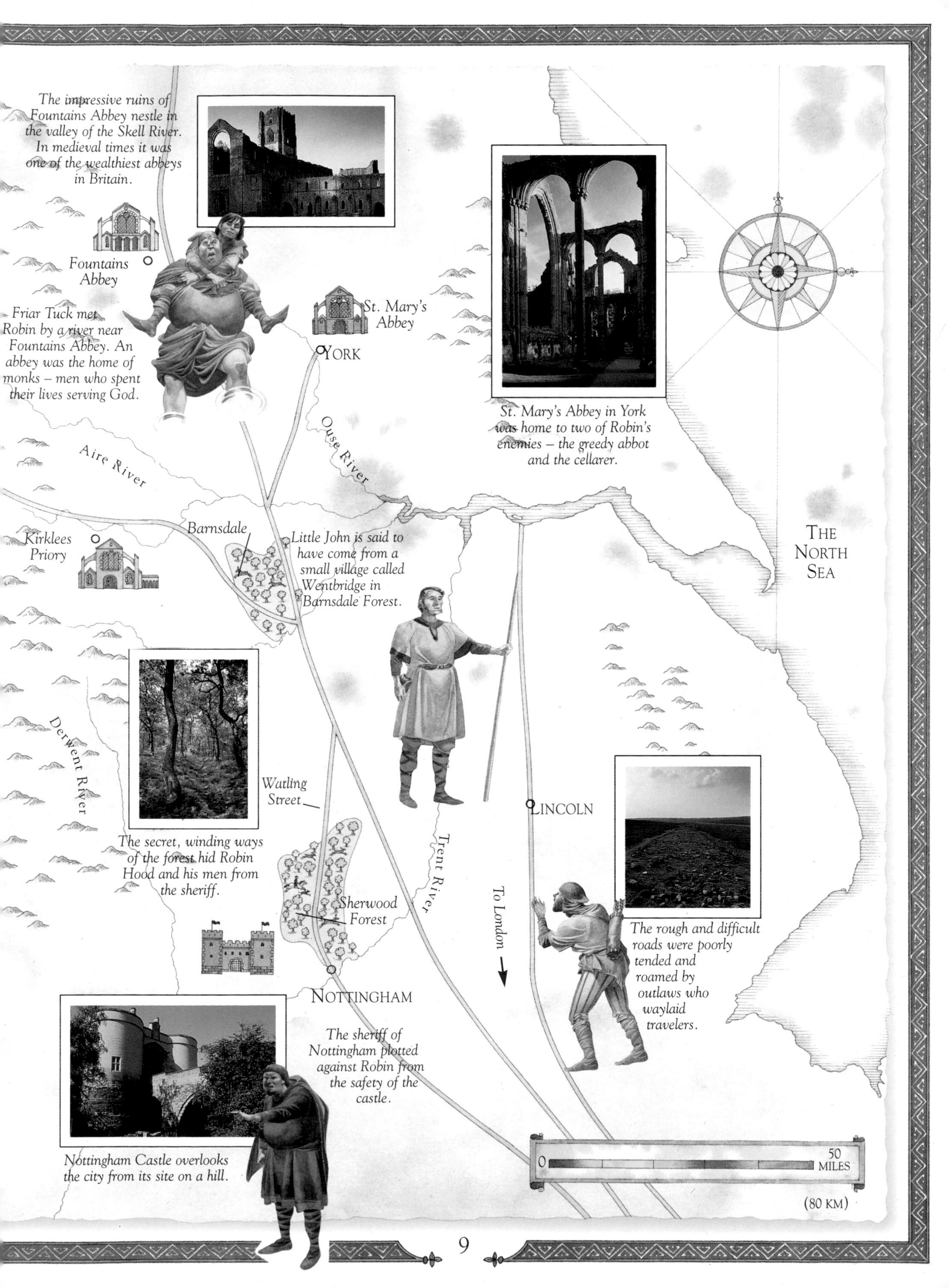
The impressive ruins of Fountains Abbey nestle in the valley of the Skell River. In medieval times it was one of the wealthiest abbeys in Britain.
Fountains Abbey
Friar Tuck met Robin by a river near Fountains Abbey. An abbey was the home of monks – men who spent their lives serving God.
St. Mary's Abbey
YORK
St. Mary's Abbey in York was home to two of Robin's enemies – the greedy abbot and the cellarer.
Aire River
Ouse River
Barnsdale
Kirklees Priory
Little John is said to have come from a small village called Wentbridge in Barnsdale Forest.
THE NORTH SEA
Derwent River
Watling Street
LINCOLN
Trent River
The secret, winding ways of the forest hid Robin Hood and his men from the sheriff.
Sherwood Forest
To London
The rough and difficult roads were poorly tended and roamed by outlaws who waylaid travelers.
NOTTINGHAM
The sheriff of Nottingham plotted against Robin from the safety of the castle.
Nottingham Castle overlooks the city from its site on a hill.
0
50 MILES
(80 KM)

THE FEUDAL SYSTEM

Robin Hood's story is set in medieval times. In western Europe at that time, people were divided into separate levels in a system called "the feudal system," based on how much land they had. The king was at the highest level, under him were the nobles, under them the knights, and under them the ordinary people.

Castles
Nobles owned castles, and the king owned many castles. Castles were secure bases from which to dominate the common people.

The king
The king owned all land. He granted important noblemen land in return for military service and complete obedience. Noblemen frequently rebelled, especially if the king was weak or absent.

The king had to travel around constantly to make his subjects do what he wanted. His court went with him; royal ladies traveled in wagons such as this.

Nobles had lots of free time to spend on their pleasures, such as hunting with hawks.

The nobles
There were many ranks within the nobility, including barons and earls, who were sometimes called lords. A noble would not normally have made friends with ordinary people. In the story, Robin, an earl, takes pride in befriending those of lower social rank.

SHERIFFS

England was divided into counties, or shires, such as Nottinghamshire. Each county had a sheriff. Sheriffs were appointed by the king from the ranks of the nobles or knights to collect taxes and carry out the decisions of the king's law courts. When the king was overseas, dishonest sheriffs could make their fortunes.

Sheriffs collected taxes and the king's other revenues.

The sheriff's men
A sheriff needed to have a number of armed men in his service to help him enforce his orders. While the king was away, the sheriff and his men sometimes took justice into their own hands.

SKILLED WORKERS

Not all peasants worked the land. Some might be stewards to knights or lords, managing their estates and finances. Some were craftspeople. Others worked as butchers, potters, or millers – one member of Robin's outlaw band was a miller's son. A few might become minstrels, singing ballads (old tales set to music) for a living.

Baker carrying loaves of bread.

Spinning
Every lord's manor produced many of its own goods, such as woolen cloth. For goods that could not be made on the manor, people had to travel to markets in towns, where potters, craftspeople, and others sold their wares.

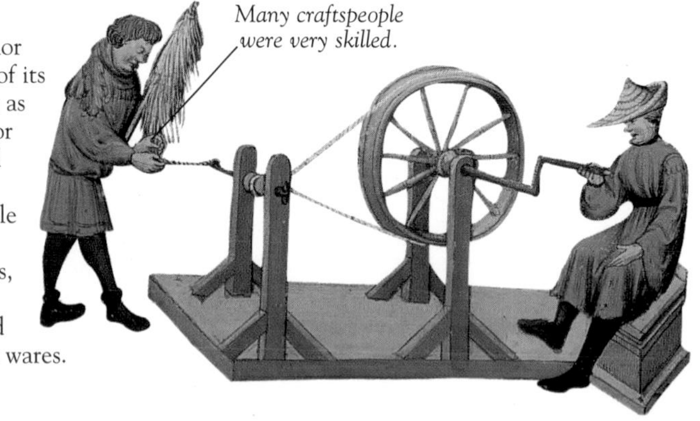

Many craftspeople were very skilled.

Baker
Towns like Nottingham developed around markets. Groups of traders, such as bakers, built shops in the same area. Others set up stalls on special market days. As they became richer, townspeople gained some power to run their own affairs.

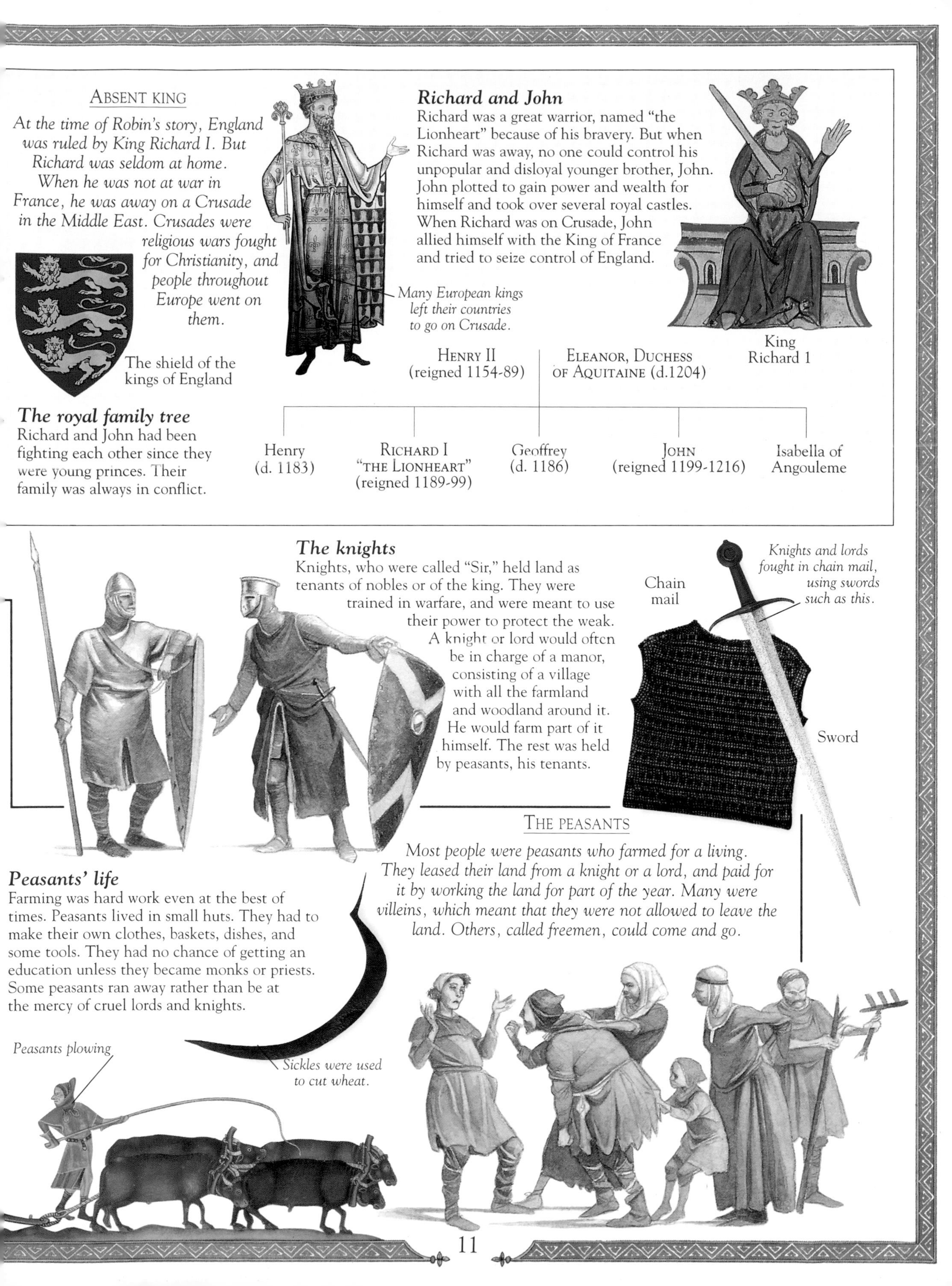

ABSENT KING

At the time of Robin's story, England was ruled by King Richard I. But Richard was seldom at home. When he was not at war in France, he was away on a Crusade in the Middle East. Crusades were religious wars fought for Christianity, and people throughout Europe went on them.

The shield of the kings of England

Many European kings left their countries to go on Crusade.

Richard and John

Richard was a great warrior, named "the Lionheart" because of his bravery. But when Richard was away, no one could control his unpopular and disloyal younger brother, John. John plotted to gain power and wealth for himself and took over several royal castles. When Richard was on Crusade, John allied himself with the King of France and tried to seize control of England.

King Richard 1

The royal family tree

Richard and John had been fighting each other since they were young princes. Their family was always in conflict.

HENRY II (reigned 1154-89) | ELEANOR, DUCHESS OF AQUITAINE (d.1204)

- Henry (d. 1183)
- RICHARD I "THE LIONHEART" (reigned 1189-99)
- Geoffrey (d. 1186)
- JOHN (reigned 1199-1216) — Isabella of Angouleme

The knights

Knights, who were called "Sir," held land as tenants of nobles or of the king. They were trained in warfare, and were meant to use their power to protect the weak. A knight or lord would often be in charge of a manor, consisting of a village with all the farmland and woodland around it. He would farm part of it himself. The rest was held by peasants, his tenants.

Chain mail

Knights and lords fought in chain mail, using swords such as this.

Sword

THE PEASANTS

Most people were peasants who farmed for a living. They leased their land from a knight or a lord, and paid for it by working the land for part of the year. Many were villeins, which meant that they were not allowed to leave the land. Others, called freemen, could come and go.

Peasants' life

Farming was hard work even at the best of times. Peasants lived in small huts. They had to make their own clothes, baskets, dishes, and some tools. They had no chance of getting an education unless they became monks or priests. Some peasants ran away rather than be at the mercy of cruel lords and knights.

Sickles were used to cut wheat.

Peasants plowing

SHERWOOD FOREST
In the year 1200, Sherwood covered about 19,000 acres (7,800 hectares) in the center of England. It was one of the largest forests in the country.

Shrinking forest
English forests now cover a much smaller area. Only 450 acres (182 hectares) of Sherwood remain.

Oak leaf

Royal hunter
Sherwood was a royal forest, reserved by the king for hunting deer and boar. Prince John loved to go hunting there, and had his own hunting lodge in the forest.

Chapter one

ROBERT OF HUNTINGDON

ONE FINE SPRING MORNING Robert, Earl of Huntingdon, went to meet his sweetheart, Marian Fitzwalter. They strolled arm-in-arm through the great forest of Sherwood until they came to a beautiful, sun-dappled glade. Robert turned toward Marian, went down on one knee, and asked, "Marian, will you be my wife?"

And Marian replied, "I will, with all my heart."

In all England there was not a more handsome pair than Robert and Marian – Maid Marian, as all the peasants called her. Standing together in the sunshine as they pledged their love, they hadn't a care in the world.

But the young lovers were not alone. For behind one of the great oaks of the forest lurked Robert's treacherous steward, Worman, who had betrayed his master and become a spy for the sheriff of Nottingham. The sheriff and Robert were sworn enemies, for the sheriff and his kind treated the poor peasants worse than cattle, and Robert felt it was his duty to defend them and treat them with respect.

Worman went running to the sheriff with the news as fast as his bandy legs would carry him. He found the fat, red-faced sheriff sitting in the gloomy great hall of Nottingham Castle, drinking wine with his henchman, Guy of Gisborne. Sir Guy, a man with evil eyes and a worse temper, did the sheriff's dirty work.

The sheriff rubbed his pudgy fingers together with glee as Worman wheezed out his news.

"So," said the sheriff, "young Robert wants to marry, does he? And he's set his heart on the fair Marian. Well, let him dream – on his wedding day we will wake him up."

The wedding was set for Midsummer's Day. In the weeks before it the young happy couple were quite content to leave all the arrangements to Worman, unaware as they were of his treachery.

Robert and Marian are overheard by Worman.

Tyrant
Sheriffs, and other powerful people, often treated the poor very badly. Peasants had little control over their own lives because they were so strictly controlled by their lords.

Timber-framed medieval house, Nottingham

Medieval town
The sheriff of Nottingham was in charge of both the town and the surrounding area. About 2,000 people lived in Nottingham. It was the largest and most important town in the district, and the center of administration.

The gatehouse is the only remaining part of the medieval castle.

Nottingham Castle
The sheriff of Nottingham lived in the castle, which was on a small hill overlooking the town. The great hall was the hub of castle life, where people drank and feasted.

Norman church
Robert and Marian probably met in a church built in the "Norman" style. Norman churches were vast and cross-shaped, with a square tower and rounded arches.

An outlaw could seek refuge in an abbey.

OUTLAW
An outlaw was someone put outside the protection of the law. Outlaws were stripped of all that they owned and banished from society. Anyone had the right to kill them.

Wolf's head
The reward for killing an outlaw was the same as the reward offered for killing a wolf. Hence it was said that an outlaw was a "wolf's head."

The day of the wedding, Robert and Marian met in church. Just as the vows were to be taken, the church doors were flung back with a crash and in strode the sheriff of Nottingham, Guy of Gisborne loping at his side, and ten armed men following after them.

"Stop the ceremony!" roared the sheriff.

"What is the meaning of this outrage?" quavered the priest.

"This man may not marry. He has been declared an outlaw. This so-called Earl of Huntingdon is a wolf's head."

"On what grounds?" shouted Robert.

"On the testimony of this man," said the sheriff, pointing to Worman. "Your steward claims you have plotted against the king."

"That is a lie," replied Robert. "Take me to the king and I will swear an oath of loyalty."

The sheriff growled.

The service was interrupted by the sheriff and his men.

"The king has left for the Crusade, there are reports that he has gone missing – either killed or captured. His brother, my friend Prince John, rules in his absence. He has outlawed you, and stripped you of your title and your lands. If King Richard comes back, you may plead for their return."

Guy of Gisborne chuckled.

"Until then," continued the sheriff, "Sir Guy here will manage your estates."

"So that is your plan," said Robert. "You call me a wolf's head, but this Sir Guy is the real wolf."

Robert turned to Marian: "My love, I know you do not love me for my title and lands. Will you still take me, now that I have nothing, not even a name?"

"I will," she said, "and I will not rest until I have cleared you of these charges. The king will return and marry us himself!"

"Then I fear nothing," said Robert. Turning, he picked up a bench and swung it, sending Sir Guy and the sheriff crashing to the floor. "The king will return, and when he does, I will accept his judgment. Until then, I will make my own laws in the greenwood. I will call myself Robin Hood – a name that you will learn to hate and fear."

"Seize him," wheezed the sheriff as he lay sprawled in the aisle. But the outlaw Robin Hood had slipped into the forest.

Royal pardon

Only the king could reverse a sentence of outlawry for crimes as serious as treason. His seal on a pardon document made it official.

Richard I's seal

Outlaws in the woods

Outlaws, thieves, and political rebels took refuge in forests such as Sherwood. The greenwood was too remote and dense for the forces of law to penetrate.

Hereward the Wake

One famous outlaw who, like Robert, took up arms against a royal intruder was Hereward the Wake. He led a rebel gang against William, Duke of Normandy, after William invaded England in 1066.

Iron arrowhead

Norman arrows

Chapter two

THE CALL OF THE FOREST

ONCE ROBIN HAD SETTLED INTO THE GREENWOOD, men flocked to his side. Many had been driven from their homes in these turbulent times or had been unjustly accused of some crime; others felt they must join Robin to fight against cruelty and injustice. And once they had found him, they had to stay with him, for every man of Robin's band was declared an outlaw.

Now Robin was still just twenty years old, and he worried that all of these men – some old enough to be his father – followed him with such blind trust, and might perhaps meet their deaths for it. So one day he went for a walk alone in the forest to think about what he should do.

Will Scarlet, one of Robin's most trusted men, begged to come with him, for the Sheriff of Nottingham had offered a reward for Robin's head, and men might even then be searching the forest for him. But Robin refused. "No man knows the forest as well as I," he said. "But I will take my horn, and blow it if I need you."

Robin walked for miles, trying to get things straight in his head. The Sheriff of Nottingham was a bully; his master Prince John was a usurper who, if he gained the throne, would prove a tyrant. The poor lived brutal lives. No woman was safe. No honest trader could sell his wares without paying bribes to the sheriff's men. Something had to be done about it.

But was it right to drag other men into what had started as a private quarrel? And could Robin expect Marian to wait for him through the long years until King Richard returned and Robin could claim his earldom again? Could it ever be right to defy the law?

As he pondered these hard questions, Robin came to a stream across which someone had laid a single plank, just wide enough for a man to cross. As Robin stepped onto the bridge, it wobbled alarmingly. He looked up, surprised out of his private thoughts, and saw that a strange man had also stepped onto the bridge, from the other side. He was a giant of a fellow, towering above Robin.

"Make way, and let me pass," said Robin.

"Make way yourself, and let me pass," the stranger replied.

Robin reached for his bow. He stared narrowly at the man. "One false move, and I'll shoot you through the heart."

"If you do, all men will call you coward," the man replied. "For you have a longbow, but I have nothing but this wooden staff to support me as I walk."

"No man will ever call me coward," said Robin. He walked into a thicket of trees, and cut an oaken staff. Then he returned to the bridge and shouted, "Now I have a staff as well. Let us see who is stronger! We will fight on this bridge and the winner will be the one who knocks the other into the water."

A strange man stepped onto the bridge.

CLOSE COMBAT
In these lawless times, people of all classes were quick to settle arguments by hand-to-hand fighting.

The quarterstaff
Blows from a quarterstaff at odd angles knocked an opponent off balance. The weapon was held a quarter of the distance from the end, hence its name.

Heavy pommel balances the long blade.

Grip

Long quillon

Double-edged, iron blade

Two-handed sword
These large, heavy swords were swung with both hands to deal a powerful blow. Quillons, or crosspieces, protected the fighter's hands from the sharp blade.

"That is my kind of fight," said the stranger, and he stepped out into the middle of the bridge.

Robin had little practice in fighting with a staff, for it was a low weapon with which peasants might settle their quarrels at a country fair. But he was a strong young man, and after all that thinking he was ready for a fight. He swung the staff, and caught the big man such a cracking blow that it made his bones ring.

The stranger swung; Robin parried. The sound of wood on wood boomed over the water.

The worst of it, thought Robin, was having to keep your balance on the narrow bridge, while dodging blows and trying to knock your opponent off at the same time. Robin could see that his lighter frame and nimbler feet were an advantage over his opponent's bulky frame. He looked the big man straight in the eye and aimed again. The stranger seemed to slip and lose his balance. Robin felt as if his blood was on fire. He lunged forward and swung his staff as hard as he could.

A smile flickered across the big man's lips as he settled his weight back on the bridge, flicked Robin's blow aside, and then cracked Robin across the head, hurling him into the water.

It was all over in seconds. As Robin disappeared beneath the stream, the big man flung aside his staff and, falling to his knees, called,

The stranger cracked Robin across the head, hurling him into the water.

"Where are you? Are you all right?"

When Robin surfaced, he was laughing. "Here I am," he said. "You are a good fighter, and a fair one, and I see that you could teach me a trick or two!"

Water warriors
Another popular combat sport was water-tilting. Two boats rowed toward each other, then the tilters on each prow attempted to knock their opponent into the water.

Practicing by tilting at a target

Fighting practice
Young men practiced their fighting skills. Those who wanted to be knights trained particularly hard to improve their physical fitness and skill with weapons.

Wrestling

Sword-and-buckler (small, wooden shield) fighting

Gymnastics

From behind every tree sprang a man in Lincoln green.

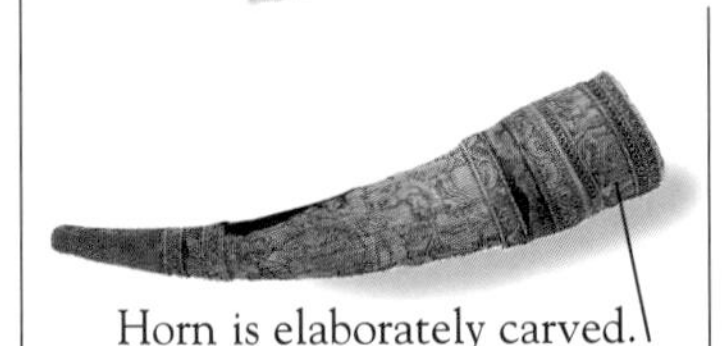
Horn is elaborately carved.

Calls for help
Horns were used for signaling during a hunt or in battle. They were usually made from hollowed-out cattle horns. When blown, they made a deep sound that carried through the thickest forest.

Huntsman blows his horn.

Robin hauled himself out onto the riverbank and, dripping everywhere, took out his horn. His warning blast rang through the forest.

In moments, half a dozen men in Lincoln green were standing at his side, Will Scarlet among them. Will was one of several former peasants who had owed their lives and loyalty to Robert, Earl of Huntingdon, and now pledged the same service to Robin Hood, Lord of the Greenwood.

"What's happened?" shouted Will. "Who is this man? If he hurt you, he shall die!" Robin's men put arrows to their bows.

"Leave him alone," laughed Robin. "A cracked head will soon mend, and no doubt I deserved it. This is a brave fellow, and I hope that he will join us."

"I can't do that," the man replied, "for I am determined to go into the forest and find the man they call Robin Hood to offer him my service."

Robin laughed again.

"You have found him," he said. "I am Robin Hood, and you are welcome to my band. What is your name, friend?"

The big man looked abashed that he had introduced himself to his new leader by hitting him over the head with a wooden staff and dunking him in a river.

"My name is John Little," he said softly.

Now it was the outlaws' turn to laugh.

"And no doubt you only drink small beer," said Will Scarlet. He turned to the others. "His mother won't let him drink anything stronger until he's fully grown."

The giant turned bright red, and Robin took pity on him.

"It's not so bad a name," he said, "but if you're going to be an outlaw, you must change it. We shall call you Little John." The men cheered, and Little John smiled.

And so it was Robin found the most faithful and good-hearted of all his men. He paid for him with a ducking and a sore head, but he never regretted the bargain. For Robin knew that if a man like Little John chose to follow him, his cause must be just and right.

For Little John was no vagabond. The only fighting he had ever done was for fun at country fairs, when he would take on all comers at wrestling or fighting with quarterstaffs. But one day at Nottingham Fair he saw Guy of Gisborne slash a peasant with his whip, shouting,

"Out of the way, you cur!"

Little John swung his mighty fist and knocked Sir Guy to the ground. And so he had become an outlaw, but his only crime was to stand up for the weak against the strong.

Servant in his master's livery

LINCOLN GREEN LIVERY
A nobleman gave his loyal servants a uniform, or livery, to wear. Robin Hood's livery was Lincoln green.

Loose hood

Lincoln green tunic

Under cover
Lincoln green was a cloth of a dull green color, making it good camouflage in the forest. It was long lasting and inexpensive.

Coloring fabric
Cloth was soaked in a mixture of yellow and blue dyes to give it its Lincoln green color.

Forest life

Forests such as Sherwood were a mixture of woodland, heath, and bog. They were not just empty woods. Peasants grazed their animals, fished, and hunted (illegally) in the forest. Wood was chopped down for use as a building material and for fuel. Some forests were quarried for stone, clay, lime, or iron. The roads were busy with travelers.

Royal forests

The kings of England created many royal forests, such as Sherwood, in which they alone could hunt. These "forests" included much farmland, and even whole villages.

The royal forests in medieval times

Forest home

Some peasants made their home in the forests, living in simple cottages like the one below. There were even a few villages in the forests.

Forest trees

If you could go back in time to the forests of Robin's day, you would see oak, birch, elm, ash, and chestnut trees. Oak was the favored timber for building in medieval England, so oaks were the only trees that were planted deliberately.

Oak tree

Berries

Acorn and leaf

Fruits of the forest

Robin and his men could pick and eat nuts, such as walnuts, hazelnuts, and chestnuts, and fruit, such as raspberries and blackberries, that grew wild in the forests.

Sweet chestnut

Mature woodland

The wood was covered with turf to keep the fire at the right temperature.

Charcoal burning

Charcoal was vital for smelting iron in medieval times. Charcoal burners needed lots of wood, so they were a familiar sight in the forests.

Peasants gathered fruit, nuts, and berries in the woods.

Peasants wore simple, homemade clothes.

Peasants

Many peasants relied on the forests for wood and for grazing, so much forest land was carefully managed. In a huge forest like Sherwood, however, there was enough wild woodland left to hide a large band of outlaws.

Hunters' prey

Hunting was the favorite sport of kings and the aristocracy. In royal forests, no one could hunt without the king's permission. The strict Forest Laws, upheld by forest courts, laid down terrible punishments for poachers (people who hunted illegally).

Boar

Wood pigeon

Stag
There were red deer, fallow deer, and roe deer in England. People also hunted wild boar and various types of birds, such as wood pigeon.

Horn
Huntsmen communicated by horn calls and hunting cries.

Wood-cutting
Wood was vital for building, firewood, fencing, and making tools. Wood-cutting was controlled by foresters.

Ax to chop down trees

Ferret

Rabbit

Ferreting
Rabbits were hunted with ferrets. All the exits of a burrow were blocked up, except for two. A ferret was sent down one of these two holes, and the rabbit ran out the other.

Poaching
The Forest Laws were much hated. Ordinary people wanted the right to hunt – they would have enjoyed hearing how Robin defied the law and poached the king's deer.

Feeding pigs
Farmers led their pigs into the forest to graze, especially in the fall, when they ate acorns.

Coppicing
Many woods were divided up into coppices. In each coppice only a few trees, or none at all, were allowed to grow to maturity. The rest were cut right back to their stumps about every 12 years. They then regrew from the stumps. This method ensured regular supplies of young wood. Some woods are still coppiced today.

Outlaws
Forests were dangerous places to travel through. Many complaints were made about the bands of outlaws and thieves hiding in the trees who robbed and killed travelers.

Robber stealing from ambushed traveler

Major Oak
Robin Hood and his outlaws are said to have camped by this oak tree in Sherwood Forest. It is one of the oldest trees in England.

Chapter three

THE CASTLE OF THE NORTH WIND

ROBIN ESTABLISHED HIS CAMP in a clearing beside a huge oak tree, with a stream running by for fresh water, and plenty of game to hunt.

Each evening, as they sat around the fire, many of his gang spoke bitterly about the sheriff and his men, living in comfort in Nottingham Castle. Robin just laughed.

"What do we need with castles of stone?" he asked. "This camp is castle enough for me, and this oak tree can be my tower. Here we can live off the land in comfort and safety. We will be more comfortable here than the sheriff in his castle; for we know where he is, but he does not know where we are."

Then Robin called for a pen, ink, and parchment, saying, "I will send the sheriff such a letter that he will never sleep soundly in his castle again."

This is what Robin wrote:

"Robin, Lord of the Greenwood, salutes the Sheriff of Nottingham. We command you, on pain of death, to cease your cruel ways. Take pity on the poor, and have mercy on those driven to steal to feed their families. If you don't, we shall harry you night and day. We shall hunt you down, even in your own castle. This I swear, by God and his blessed Mother, and in the name of King Richard. Given at our Castle of the North Wind, in the merry month of May."

Robin settled himself on the branch of an oak and started to write a letter to the sheriff.

Robin's men burst into laughter. Much, the miller's son, who was unknown in Nottingham, said, "I shall deliver the letter into the sheriff's hands myself."

The next morning, Much set off to Nottingham with the letter. Robin and his men spent the morning practicing archery. Little John, having the longest reach and the strongest arms, could shoot the farthest. Robin said, "I would go a long way to see the man who could outshoot you, Little John."

Will Scarlet said, "You would not have to go far. A friar at Fountains Abbey is the strongest bowman in this land – Brother Michael Tuck is his name."

"Then we must go and see this mighty man of God," said Robin.

Robin and six of his men made their way to Fountain Dale, and there, by the riverbank, they saw the friar. He was not as tall as Little John, but what he lacked in height he made up in girth. He was nearly completely round.

Robin laughed. "These friars certainly feed themselves well," he said. He told his men to hide behind a bank of ferns, but to come to his aid if he blew his horn.

Robin walked along the river until he came to the friar, who was dressed in his religious habit, but with a sword strapped to his side, a shield in his hands, and a steel helmet on his head.

"Are the friars to go to war with the monks, Father?" asked Robin.

"No, my son. But I find it concentrates my mind on my prayers if I practice my skill at arms."

"Well, today you have the chance to do a good deed that will please God more than swordplay. I want to cross the river without getting wet, so just carry me over there will you?"

The friar hoisted Robin onto his back, and carried him through the fast and cold water. On the far side, Robin began to walk away.

"Not so fast!" called the friar, drawing his sword. "Now you have the chance to do me a good turn. I want to cross back to the other side again, and you can do the carrying."

Robin could scarcely lift the fat friar, and his knees started to buckle under the strain. He plunged forward through the water, and just made it to the far side before his legs gave way.

Letter
Robin's letter is based on an actual letter written to a parson by "Lionel, King of the Rout of Raveners (robbers)," in 1336.

Parchment

Quill pen

Fountains Abbey
Friar Tuck stayed at Fountains Abbey, Yorkshire, the ruins of which still stand today. It had been set up by monks from St. Mary's Abbey in York, seeking a more spiritual life.

Friars
Friars were religious men who wandered from place to place teaching people about the life of Christ. They vowed to spend their lives in poverty.

This time Robin drew his sword. "Carry me back!" he ordered. Sighing, the friar lifted Robin up again. Halfway across, he shrugged his shoulders and sent Robin tumbling into the stream.

"Sink or swim," he shouted, "I'll not be your beast of burden."

Robin swam to the far side as the friar backed away.

Robin took out his bow and fired arrows at the friar, but he turned them away with his shield. "Shoot on, I have nothing else to do, and this is good practice."

Robin, speechless with anger, plunged back across the river, sword in hand, and swung wildly at the mocking friar. The friar matched him blow for blow. No matter how hard he tried, Robin could not beat him. Weakened by the friar's blows, Robin cried, "Wait, wait! Let me give one blow on my horn."

Robin blew, and Little John, Will Scarlet, and the others all tumbled out from behind the ferns.

"Wait, wait!" cried the friar. "Let me whistle once."

The friar whistled, and six savage dogs came running to his call.

"A dog for every man," said the friar, "and you for myself."

The dogs set on the men before they could draw their bows, and began to rip at their clothes.

"Hold, hold!" shouted Robin. The friar whistled again, and the dogs retreated.

"You are truly a warrior," said Robin, "and the man for us. I am Robin Hood and these are my men. Join us in the forest and be our priest. You shall eat well, I assure you – we live off the king's deer, and the sheriff's coffers."

"Very well, I'll come," said the friar. "My name is Friar Tuck, and I vow to serve you and your outlaw band as priest for as long as you reign in the forest – and there's venison to eat."

When they got back to camp, Much had returned from his

The ice-cold water chilled the fat friar's calves.

Fighting dog
Fierce dogs, such as this mastiff, were used to hunt wolves, and were pitched against one another in dog fights. The most savage dogs were used in battle.

Criminal clergymen
From 1417 to 1429, Robert Stafford, a Sussex priest, led a band of outlaws using the alias "Friar Tuck."

journey to Nottingham.

"Well," asked Robin, "did the sheriff get his letter?"

"Yes," Much replied, "I put it into his hand myself."

"How did he like it?"

"His face turned yellow, then red, then purple, and he started to choke. Guy of Gisborne had to hit him on the back. As I made my escape, I could hear him bellowing, 'Where is the Castle of the North Wind?'"

"Where indeed?" said Robin, "For the wind blows where it wills, and no man can command it."

Belted friar
The name "Tuck" does not refer to "tucking" into food. A "tuck" was the rope-belt worn around a Franciscan friar's waist.

Rope-belt worn by St. Francis

The dogs set on the men and began to rip at their clothes.

Religious life

Norman church, built in 1150

In Robin Hood's day, the religion of western Europe was Roman Catholicism. Almost everyone belonged to "the church," the Christian community. The church owned a great deal of land and church leaders were very powerful. Some used their power and wealth to help the needy, others seemed only interested in obtaining more land and riches.

House of prayer

Churches were always left open so that Christians could go in to pray or confess their sins. Many churches were built during the period in which the story was se

Chapels were small churches that were part of a house or monastery.

Church life

Men and women accepted the teachings of the church, and tried to live their lives according to Christian values. Many people went to church on Sundays and on holy days, such as Christmas.

Priests and people

Priests were responsible for making sure that people understood Christian teachings.

Marriage

Priests led the marriage service, at which husband and wife publicly promised to be faithful to each other. Usually people were married in church, or in the church porch, but a priest could conduct a wedding anywhere, even in a forest, if necessary.

Baptizing

Babies were baptized, or christened, soon after birth. Baptism marked their entry into the Christian community. In the ceremony, holy water was poured over them to symbolize God's love and forgiveness.

Wealth of the church

The church was very powerful and wealthy and owned a lot of land. Churches were often richly decorated.

Medieval jeweled cross

Monks and priests were almost the only people who could read and write.

This medieval gold ring belonged to a pope.

Making wine

Monks often made beer and wine, some of it very fine. The monk in charge of the cellar where the wine and beer was stored was called the cellarer.

Herb garden

Marjoram

Medieval medicine

Monks and nuns often cared for the sick. Herbs that were used in medicine, such as marjoram and feverfew, were grown in monastery and priory gardens.

Feverfew

The Religious Community

Many men and women lived in religious communities called monasteries, abbeys, or priories. They were supposed to devote their lives to prayer and serving others.

Church leaders

The pope was the head of the Catholic Church. Then came cardinals, followed by archbishops and then bishops.

Monks

Each order (group) of monks had its own uniform. Monks and friars had tonsures (round bald patches). Like the special clothes, the tonsure was a sign that they were set apart to serve God and other people.

Abbot

The head of a monastery was called an abbot or a prior. He was meant to be like a father to the other monks.

Friar

Friars traveled all over Europe, helping the poor, preaching, and teaching.

Nun

A community of nuns was led by an abbess or prioress.

Monastic life

A community of monks was self-sufficient, with its own church, hospital, and gardens.

Travelers

Monks always had a bed for the poor, the sick, pilgrims, or ordinary travelers such as these.

OUTDOOR FEAST
Under the much-hated Forest Laws, hunting and feasting in royal forests was legal only with royal permission. Robin and his men could be hanged if caught defying the law.

The herb sage adds flavor to venison.

Pouring fat over the meat

Roasting
Deer meat, called venison, was put on a long spit over a charcoal fire and turned slowly. Fat was poured over the meat to prevent it from drying out and burning.

Little John went down on one knee to welcome the traveler to the forest.

Chapter four

A GUEST AT THE FEAST

AS ROBIN INHALED the appetizing smell of deer roasting over an open fire, he said, "What a shame we have no guest to share our meal."

"Or to pay for it," quipped Will Scarlet.

"What a wonderful idea," said Robin. "Why don't you take Little John and Much and look for a traveler who might be glad to pay for a hot meal as he journeys through the greenwood?"

So Will and the others went to

watch over the forest path, at a point where the outlaws often held up travelers, taxing the rich for their passage, but letting the honest and poor go for free.

At last a knight came riding down the path.

"I don't think much of this one," said Little John. "If he were a fish, I would throw him back."

And indeed the man was a sorry sight, in travel-stained clothes, with one foot in his stirrup and the other dangling weakly by his horse's side. But though his clothes were poor, his back was straight and his chin jutted proudly before him.

Will replied, "We have found rich pickings before under poorer cloaks than that."

The three outlaws leaped out onto the path. Much caught hold of the horse's bridle, while Will Scarlet shouted, "Stop, in the name of Robin Hood."

"Mind your manners, Will." Little John said. "This gentleman is to be our guest." Then, with a flourish, the outlaw went down on one huge knee, saying, "Welcome to the forest, kind sir. Please accompany us to our camp, where lunch awaits you."

They brought the knight to the outlaws' camp, where Robin welcomed him. "Sit down," he said, "and eat and drink your fill. Would you like some of the king's roast deer? Or perhaps you would care for some humble pie, instead?"

The knight looked straight into Robin's eyes. "I will be eating humble pie enough, my friend, in the days to come. Give me some roast deer, if you will."

"I see there is some story here." Robin replied.

After the knight and the outlaws had eaten and drunk their fill, Robin said, "Before you go on your way, sir knight, I must ask you to pay for your dinner."

The knight replied, "I wish that I could, but I have nothing to pay you with – only a few pennies that I need for my journey." Little John looked in the man's saddlebag, and he was telling the truth.

"I will not take a penny," said Robin, "but tell me, sir, how you come to be in such a poor state?"

Poor food

"Humble pie" was made from a deer's entrails. These unappetizing pies were inexpensive and were eaten by poor people.

Drink

The outlaws would have drunk beer, made from barley, or wine with their meals. They were not used to drinking water as it was often unsafe.

Barley

Wine and beer were normally stored in barrels.

Travelers in danger

In the 12th century, Sherwood Forest was well known for being a hideout for bands, like Robin's, that ambushed travelers.

Stylish knight

Knights did not always wear shining armor. Sir Richard's rags showed he had fallen on hard times.

"My name is Sir Richard of the Lee," said the knight, "and once I was a wealthy man. But my son took part in a tournament, and by an unlucky stroke killed a knight of Lancaster. It has taken all my money to buy his freedom, and I have had to borrow four hundred pounds from the abbot of St. Mary's, with my own estate as security. Now the loan is due, and I cannot repay it. I am going to plead with the abbot for more time."

"Your pleading will not get you far with that one," said Robin. "He has lain his greedy hands on many estates before yours."

"What else can I do?" asked the knight.

"Why," said Robin, "you can pay the man his money."

And with that Robin fetched four hundred pounds from a secret place and gave it to Sir Richard.

"I will pay you back," stammered Sir Richard. "I swear it by Our Lady."

"I know you will," said Robin. "But for now, God speed you on your journey! Little John shall see you safe through the forest, and I shall expect to see you again in a year and a day." And with that, the knight rode off.

Tournaments

Knights trained for war in mock battles called tournaments. Any knight who killed another was thrown into prison by their victim's lord.

Buying freedom

The imprisoned knight's family had to pay a heavy ransom to buy his freedom. The families of common criminals could also buy their freedom by paying a fine to the judge or the family of their victims.

Some prisoners were kept locked in manacles.

Money

There were 240 pennies to the English pound. One pound might buy a cow or a horse. Four hundred pounds was the price of a large country manor.

Groat worth four pennies

Gold coin, called a noble, was worth 80 pennies

In the abbey, the abbot was rubbing his hands.

"It is the day for Sir Richard of the Lee to repay his loan or lose his lands," he said. "Where is he? He has not come, and in a few hours his lands will be mine forever."

The cellarer of the abbey answered, "The man is probably dead, or hanged. Have a cup of wine against the cold."

The abbot cackled with glee as the rich wine warmed him.

At that moment, there was a rapping on the door. It was Sir Richard, asking to see the abbot. He laid out his sword and kneeled. When the abbot saw the knight's worn clothing, he thought the lands were his for sure.

The abbot and cellarer laughed as Sir Richard kneeled before them.

Abbot
Abbots often loaned money to landowners who could forfeit their estates if they failed to pay it back. Greedy abbots set impossible repayment dates so they could get the land and the rents of the tenants living on it.

Good wine was kept locked away.

Cellarer
The cellarer was in charge of food and drink in the abbey, particularly the abbey's wine cellar. Wine was used in religious services and at meals.

Our Lady
Like many people of the time, Robin and Sir Richard were devoted to Mary (Our Lady). Robin believes there is "no greater promise" than Sir Richard's, as it was sworn by Our Lady.

Mary, mother of Jesus, is the subject of many works of art.

St. Mary's Abbey
St. Mary's Abbey was founded in 1086 by the Benedictine order of monks. The abbey became one of the wealthiest in Britain. It acquired large areas of land, used to rear sheep for wool, Britain's main export. The abbot lived in such a grand style that in 1132 some monks left to found Fountains Abbey in protest.

"Well, have you the money?" asked the abbot.

"I have tried hard," said Sir Richard, "but I have not been able to raise it. Please allow me more time."

"Your time is up," said the abbot. "If you can't pay, you can't pay."

"I didn't say that," said Sir Richard, rising to his feet and shaking out the four hundred pounds. "All of the money is there," he said, and left, leaving the abbot and the cellarer scrambling on the floor for the scattered coins.

A year and a day later, Robin and his men waited in Sherwood for Sir Richard, who was due to repay his loan. Robin said, "I fear some mischief may have befallen Sir Richard, for I expected him sooner."

"Don't you worry that he won't pay you back?" asked Will Scarlet.

"Never," said Robin. "He swore by Our Lady, and there is no greater promise than that. Go to the path and see if Sir Richard is coming, and tell him his lunch is ready."

Will, Little John, and Much the miller's son went looking. But instead of the knight, they saw two monks in black habits riding along the forest path. The outlaws invited them to lunch.

As they sat down to dine, Robin asked the monks,

"Which abbey are you from?"

The abbot had his own market, fair, prison, and gallows on abbey land.

Cloister

Kitchen

Common parlor

Hospitium, or guest house

"St. Mary's," replied the first monk. "I am the cellarer."

"That is a shame," said Robin. "I had hoped that you had been sent with money, for you serve Our Lady, and she has promised me repayment of a loan this very day."

"I am carrying no money," said the monk. "Just a few pennies for my traveling expenses."

"If what you say is true," said Robin, "I will not take a penny from you. Little John, take a look in their saddlebags."

Little John opened the monk's saddlebags, and found more than eight hundred pounds in gold.

"I see you have brought my money, after all, in double measure," said Robin. "I thank you for the service."

And then he sent the crestfallen monks on their way.

That evening, a rider came into Robin's camp. It was Sir Richard. "Forgive me, friend, for leaving you waiting all day. On my way to see you, I came upon a wrestling match. A poor man, who had the prize, was being cheated of his right by a group of sneering nobles. I had to stay and put the matter right."

"To help the poor is the first duty of any man," said Robin Hood.

"I have brought you back the money you lent me," said Sir Richard, "with thanks from the bottom of my heart."

"But I have already been repaid," said Robin. "Our Lady sent the cellarer of her abbey with eight hundred pounds this very day. But really, the overpayment is too much. So here is four hundred pounds back. I know you will use it to help the poor on your lands."

Sir Richard took the money with thanks, and then he said, "I thought long and hard for a gift to bring you. You have saved my lands for me, but I cannot give you back your lands, or your name. So I have brought you a yew longbow and a set of arrows trimmed with peacock feathers. May they never miss their mark!"

Abbot's grand house

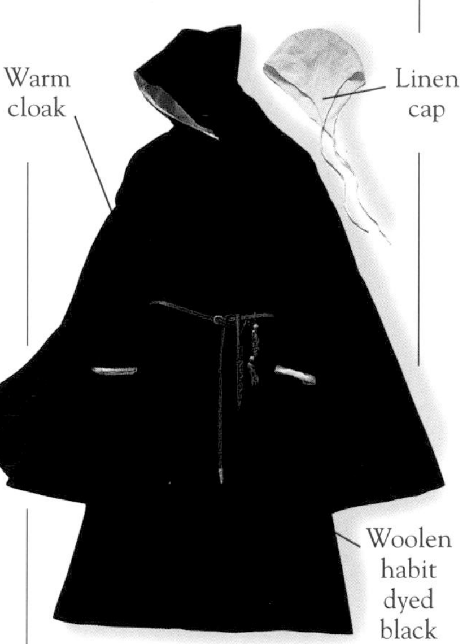

Monks' habits
Benedictines were known as the Black Monks because they wore black habits. These plain clothes reflected monks' vows to remain poor. The monks in the story, however, are looking after hundreds of pounds.

Charity
It was part of a nobleman's duty to help the poor who lived on their estates. They gave them small cash gifts or, after a feast, arranged for leftovers to be given to the needy.

Chapter five

THE ARCHERY CONTEST

ALL THIS TIME, as Robin and his men took the king's deer for free and laughed at the law, the sheriff of Nottingham was plotting his revenge.

"You must lure Robin into a trap," advised Sir Guy of Gisborne.

"I see that," said the sheriff, "but what trap would be cunning enough to catch someone as wily as Robin Hood?"

Hearing the story of Sir Richard, and how he had given Robin a magnificent longbow, the sheriff struck the table with his fist. "I have it," he shouted. "We will hold an archery competition. All the bowmen in Nottinghamshire will come and strive to see who is the best shot of all. The prize shall be an arrow made of pure silver, with feathers and a head of gold. Robin will never resist such a lure."

And it is true that when Robin heard of the competition, he longed to take part. But how could he? As soon as he showed his face in Nottingham, he would be captured.

It was a moody Robin who joined his men at the bend in the road where they waylaid travelers passing through the forest. The dust of a cart appeared in the distance. Little John said, "It is just the potter going to market, as he has done these past three years. Let him pass."

"Three years!" said Robin. "You mean this churl has been using our path for three years and never paid a penny's toll?" As the cart approached, Robin leaped out and caught hold of the horse.

"Let go!" said the potter.

"Not until you have paid a toll," said Robin.

"Who are you, that I should pay you a toll?"

"I am Robin Hood."

"In that case," said the potter, "I will be happy to pay." Getting down from his cart, he swung his fist, knocking Robin over. "There you are," he said, climbing back into his cart. "I will be happy to pay such a toll every time I pass."

Robin leaped up and they began to fight in earnest, exchanging blows and wrestling in the dust.

Busy roads
As towns like Nottingham grew, so did the amount of local road traffic. Merchants, noblemen, and pilgrims made rich pickings for Robin's men.

Making pots
Like many craftsmen, potters worked at home, then brought their goods by road to markets in local towns.

Carts
Goods such as pottery were carried by simple carts drawn by horses or oxen.

Rope holds gate shut.

Large wheels ride over bumps and ruts.

Wheel is clad with iron for strength.

Shafts for pulling the cart

At last Little John emerged from hiding and pulled them apart.

"You are a man to reckon with," said Robin. "You may drive through the forest every day, and I shall never charge a toll again!"

The potter laughed, "Then let us be friends, outlaw, and if I can be of help to you, you only have to ask. And now, I shall be on my way – I don't want to miss the archery competition."

Robin said, "Neither do I. Why not change clothes with me? Stay here, and my men will serve you a feast fit for a king – and I will go to Nottingham disguised in your clothes."

"As long as you don't forget to sell my pots," said the potter, and the deal was struck.

Toll road

Local landowners charged a small fee, or toll, to anyone traveling on their roads to pay for their upkeep. Robin jokes that the money he robs from travelers is a toll.

Robin leaped out and caught hold of the horse.

NATIONAL PASTIME
Archery was a popular sport, and competitions were common. Usually, archers aimed to split a wooden mark fixed to a target.

Robin hid his bow and arrows in the potter's cart and drove into Nottingham, as cool as you please. He found himself a good position right by the practice ground where the competition was to take place, and was soon doing brisk business. Robin so enjoyed shouting out, "Pots for sale! Best pots in Nottinghamshire!" that he almost forgot about shooting in the competition.

Archers from all around were taking part, and many of them were fine archers indeed. But Robin saw that none of them were his match. He sold his last five pots to the sheriff's wife, and said to her, "Though I am but a humble potter, I would love to try my hand for the silver arrow. I have a bow in my cart that someone gave me as a present. Will I be allowed to enter?"

"I am sure that anyone can enter who has a bow to shoot with," said the sheriff's wife, so Robin took his place at the end of the line.

The crowd was silent as the first archer shot his arrow at the target. This man was known locally as an expert archer, and many had bet good money that he would take the prize. Few archers could match him for accuracy at such a distance, and with so many eyes on them.

The arrow hit the mark, and as it thrummed in the central circle, the watchers erupted into cheers.

No other archer shot as well. Some even missed the target altogether, to jeers and catcalls of the crowd. Then Robin stepped up, and strung his bow. Robin calmed his mind, emptying it of everything except the arrow and the target. He fired, and sent his arrow whistling into the wooden marker dead in the middle, splitting it into three even pieces.

"Well shot," shouted the sheriff's wife, and even the sheriff himself clapped politely, though he was sick at heart that his plan had not worked. Robin Hood had not turned up, and now he had to give the precious silver arrow, which had cost him a fortune, to a mere potter.

Nevertheless, he handed over the prize.

"That was a fine shot, fellow," he said. "Someone bring me the arrow he fired, so that I can see how it was fletched."

Robin said, "I thank your honor for your kind words, and for this silver arrow, but I must be on my way. There is no rest for a poor man in these times."

And with that Robin climbed back in the cart and began to drive off as fast as he could. If he was not clear of the gates before the sheriff guessed who he was, he could be shut in the city, and trapped like an animal. Robin was just at the gates when the stewards brought his winning arrow to the sheriff.

"This is a fine arrow, indeed," said the sheriff.

"Look how well it is made. The fletcher has even used peacock feathers, not goose quills."

And then the sheriff remembered the story of Sir Richard's present to Robin Hood, and realized that he had been tricked.

"Guards! Guards!" he shouted. "Stop that potter!"

But Robin Hood was already past the gates, on his way back to the safety of the greenwood, while the sheriff was left to nurse his injured pride.

Robin split the marker into three even pieces.

Prize arrows
The sheriff saw that Robin's arrows were feathered, or fletched, with peacocks' feathers. These were rarer and more valuable than goose feathers, with which arrows were normally made. The feathered part of an arrow is called the vane.

Vane

Shaft

Walled town
If an outlaw was found inside a town, the people chasing him would shout to warn the gatekeepers to shut the gate. The outlaw would be caught, trapped within the town walls.

Archery

Robin Hood was a skilled archer.

The longbow became the most common weapon in medieval England. This weapon, as tall as its user, could send a lethal arrow 200 yards (180 meters). Kings encouraged archery because archers were the most effective members of the English army. King Edward III (1327–77) even made archery practice compulsory on Sundays and feast days. All Englishmen had at least some knowledge of archery, and the best archers were well-known and widely admired, but none was as famous as Robin Hood.

The nock, usually made of horn, holds the string in place.

Yew bow

Bowstring

It took great effort to pull the string back.

Crossbow

Crossbows

Crossbows were easier to use than longbows and more accurate at close range (unless the longbowmen were very skillful). But they did not fire as far and they took much longer to reload. They shot small arrows called bolts or quarrels.

Crossbow-man preparing to fire

Shaft of arrow

Making the Bow

Bows were made by a craftsman called a bowyer. They were usually made from the wood of the yew tree, which was light and strong. First, logs of yew were cut into thin sections called bowstaves. The bowstaves were then stored for three or four years to "season" them – a bow made from "young" (new) wood would not shoot properly. Then the bowyer shaped the staves into slender bows.

Leaf from yew tree

Strings and arrows

Bowstrings were made of twine, which was made from hemp and flax plants (below). Ash was perhaps the most sought-after wood for arrows, though they could be made from many types of wood. Feathers were stuck on with glue made from bluebell bulbs.

Shaping the bowstave

Bluebell

Hemp

Flax

Archery

It took years of practice to become a good archer. Robin must have had very strong muscles just to draw the bowstring back and hold it steady as he aimed. The best archers were incredibly accurate, and could shoot up to 16 arrows a minute.

Goose feather

Longbow arrow

Crossbow bolt

Arrowheads

Arrowheads were made of iron or steel and had different shapes for different uses. Broadheads were used for hunting, narrower heads were used in battle to penetrate armor.

Broadhead

Feathers

Arrows could have feathers glued and tied to their ends to make them fly straighter. Usually the flight feathers of geese were used; arrows with peacock feathers, such as Robin was given, were rare and special.

BATTLES

In battle, nobles fought as mounted knights. Ordinary people fought as archers and footsoldiers. Skilled bowmen could defeat even the best knights. English bowmen won many battles for their country against their traditional enemy, France.

Longbows were used by the English against the French in the Battle of Agincourt, 1415.

Grip protects hand as bowstring lashes across it.

Archers at practice

Men practiced archery throughout Europe. Targets were set up on earthen mounds, called butts. Anything could be used as a target, even a piece of wood.

Target

Earthen mound, or butt

Archery became a very competitive sport.

A longbow was about as long as its user was tall.

MODERN-DAY ARCHERY

Modern-day Robin Hoods can take part in the Olympic Games. Archery is a thriving sport. The bows are a little different, but the skill remains the same.

A modern archer takes aim.

Hunting

Longbows were sometimes used by the rich for hunting on their estates. Wealthy women learned to hunt, too. This medieval picture shows Diana, the Greek goddess of hunting. Maid Marian may well have used a bow herself.

Red deer

A WOMAN'S PLACE
Upper-class women, like Marian, had little power to make decisions. Their fathers decided whom they should marry, so anyone who had power over the fathers had power over the daughters as well.

Wide-sleeved gowns were worn by rich ladies.

Chapter six

FLIGHT TO THE FOREST

WHILE ROBIN WAS LIVING in Sherwood, gathering men to follow him, Marian was living quietly at home with her father, Lord Fitzwalter. She had sworn to wait for Robin, and wait she would, though she had never thought the wait would be so long. Would King Richard never come home?

The sheriff of Nottingham had left her alone so far, but now that Robin had tricked him at the archery contest, his anger boiled over. He told Sir Guy of Gisborne that if Guy could kill or capture Robin, he could have Robin's lands and title for himself, and any other reward he wanted.

"What about Robin's bride-to-be?" leered Sir Guy.

"If you want her, you can have her," said the sheriff.

"Then let us go and tell her the happy news," said Sir Guy.

They rode to Lord Fitzwalter's house with a troop of armed men, and burst in on him and Marian at their private prayers.

"What is the meaning of this?" spluttered the angry lord.

"It could have several meanings," replied the sheriff coolly. "It could mean treason, and black conspiracy against Prince John and the officers of the king's law. It could mean outlawry. It could mean the gallows. But these are unpleasant meanings, meanings we need not concern ourselves with. Instead let us look on the bright side, and say that this visit means joy and celebration, and the longed-for union of two young lovers."

"Lovers?"

"Why, is your daughter Marian not pining to get married?"

"You know she is."

"Then she shall. She shall marry the Earl of Huntingdon."

"But how? Robert, Earl of Huntingdon has been outlawed, by your own command."

"I do not speak of that common criminal Robin Hood. How could you think of allying your family to such a scoundrel? I speak of good

Women's work
At home, Marian would have spent her days learning the duties of a wife. These included managing household money and servants, and spinning and weaving clothes.

Loom

Ladies make wool ready for weaving.

Sir Guy here, who has long admired your daughter. I have charged Sir Guy with the arrest of Robin Hood. And when Robin Hood is swinging from the gallows, I will confirm Sir Guy in the title of Earl of Huntingdon, and the possession of all that wicked felon's lands. What better could you hope for than that your daughter should become Sir Guy's loving wife?"

"No!" shouted Lord Fitzwalter. "It's absurd!"

"I would advise you not to take that line," said the sheriff, "or I might tell Prince John how you and your daughter have plotted with Robin Hood against the realm. Sir Guy can become Lord Fitzwalter as easily as Earl of Huntingdon. And I do not think you, my lord, with your creaking limbs, would make a happy outlaw in the forest. And do you want to see the proud Maid Marian reduced to an outlaw's wench? Think about it."

As the sheriff and Sir Guy took their leave, Sir Guy placed his hand on Marian's cheek, and said, "Do not keep me waiting long, my sweet."

Private chapel
Rich families had a chapel attached to their home with room for them and their servants to pray in.

Sir Guy placed his hand on Marian's cheek.

FORTIFIED HOME
Families such as Marian's lived in manor houses, which had strong stone walls for defense. A lord of the manor owned all the local land – village, meadows, and woods.

As the door closed behind them, Marian turned to her father. Her face was white except for the red marks of Sir Guy's fingers, and she was shaking with fury.

"Father! How dare they?"

"They dare because they have the power to do what they threaten. They can strip me of my title and lands, and without them, who am I and who are you? Just two more vagabonds whom the sheriff can dispose of as he likes. Who is there to protect the likes of us?"

"There is my Robin," said Maid Marian, her voice trembling with pride. "He would look after us, I know he would."

"But the sheriff was right, my dear. I am too old and too ill to live in the greenwood. It is not summer all year round, and once the harsh winter came and the cold and wet seeped into my clothes, my end would not be far off. If I leave this manor, where I can lie on a goose-feather bed, eat three meals a day, and sit by the fire in the evening to warm my old bones, I will not see another spring."

"But I am young and fit. And with my Robin at my side, no winter wind could chill me. Father, let me go to him. You know he is a man of honor. And once I am gone, how can the sheriff act against you? Promise Sir Guy my hand, if you like, but he will have to find me first."

"You are right, Marian. But how can you escape? The sheriff will have posted men to watch for such a move."

"Do not ask, Father, and then when the sheriff asks you, you will not know. But do not worry about me. I am not afraid of the sheriff

Chapel
Gatehouse
Tower
Moat
Well
Solar, lord's private room
Great hall
Kitchens
Side gate
Accommodation for important householders

Manor house
The heart of the manor was the great hall, where everyone ate. The lord curtained off one end to make a private room, containing his big bed.

Vagabond
Vagabonds were people who fled their village without their lord's permission. They wandered from place to place, carrying out petty crimes.

or his men, and I know the hidden ways of the greenwood as well as Robin himself."

Next morning at dawn, Marian dressed as a page boy heading off on some household errand. She slipped from her room and out across the courtyard, past the hall, before reaching the side gate. Easing it open, she tiptoed across the creaking wooden moat bridge and walked quickly down the path. When she reached the trees, she ran into the safety of the forest.

When the sheriff and Sir Guy arrived at the house, Marian was long gone.

"Where is she? When did she go?" screamed the sheriff.

Lord Fitzwalter could only say, "My lord, I do not know. I told her that I was going to promise her in marriage to Sir Guy, as you suggested, and she must have fled. But do not worry. A mere slip of a girl will not get far. Surely you had men posted outside?"

The sheriff called in his spies and asked them if any of them had seen Maid Marian leave. The one who had been watching the side door said, "No, sir, I did not. No one left but a page boy, at dawn."

"A page boy! You dunderhead! You stupid oaf! Maid Marian is as slim as a willow wand. Dress her in boy's clothes and she would pass as a boy anywhere. Follow her!"

But the sheriff's men could not follow Marian's tracks through the secret forest ways and they soon lost her trail.

And so it was that later that day a new recruit arrived at Robin's camp. He was taken to Robin, who, looking at the boy before him, said, "You are too young for this dangerous life. Go back home, and join us when you are older."

The page boy replied, "My home is here with you, my dear."

And so saying he took off his cap and unpinned his hair. As the golden locks came tumbling down, Robin exclaimed, "Marian!"

The lovers fell into each other's arms, overjoyed at their reunion. That night the outlaws held a feast to welcome Marian to their camp, and they drank many a toast to "Robin and Marian! Marian and Robin! Robin and Marian!"

Page boys would serve the lords and ladies at table.

Page boy
Boys aged about seven who were going to be knights were sent to a nobleman's house to be trained. Pages were taught good manners, how to serve a knight, and how to attend to ladies.

In disguise
Robin Hood was a master of disguises and so was Marian, who dressed up as a page boy to escape to Robin in the forest.

Romantic moment
Robin and Marian reunite in this 1991 movie version starring Kevin Costner and Mary Elizabeth Mastrantonio.

Butcher
Butchers bought animals from farmers and killed them to sell at market. Only the town's rich people, such as the sheriff's wife, could afford to buy meat.

Shopping center
All over Europe, market towns were growing up. Merchants built shops in the town center. On market day, traders came to town and set up stalls.

A shop's sign was a symbol of its trade. This sheaf of wheat is a baker's sign.

French market containing shops with built-in stalls

Chapter seven

THE MASTER BUTCHER

WHEN MAID MARIAN TOLD ROBIN all about the sheriff's threats, he said, "This man must be taught a lesson." So Robin changed clothes with a butcher, and went once more to market in Nottingham.

He set up his stall, and was soon doing a roaring trade, for he sold more meat for a penny than the other butchers did for three. He even sold meat to the sheriff's wife, giving her a prime cut for free. She was so pleased that she allowed him and the other butchers to dine at the sheriff's hall.

When they sat down to eat, Robin said grace:

"May God make us able
To eat all at the table!"

All the butchers laughed. This young rascal seemed harmless enough. And when Robin said, "I'll pay for everyone," and slapped five pounds on the table, they were ready to forgive him anything.

The sheriff, seeing the young man throwing his money about, thought, "This is some young fool, and a fool and his money are soon parted." So he engaged the young butcher in conversation.

"Tell me," said the sheriff, "do you have horned beasts for sale?" He meant cattle.

"That I do," said Robin. "Two or three hundred. And a hundred acres of land. Do you know what they might be worth?"

The sheriff offered Robin half the true value, "Three hundred pounds."

"Then come with me, and bring the money," said Robin, "and if you like the beasts and the land, we can do a deal."

It was all the sheriff could do not to drool down his chin at the thought of the wonderful bargain he was getting.

So the sheriff mounted a palfrey, and he and Robin rode out of town. "The path leads through the forest," said Robin.

"God protect us from Robin Hood," answered the sheriff.

As they went deep into Sherwood, they came across a herd of a hundred red deer. "Here are some of my horned beasts," said Robin. "How do you like them?"

"What do you mean, fellow? These are the king's deer! And where are your hundred acres?"

"Why, we have been riding through them. All Sherwood is mine, if it is any man's." With that, Robin blew three blasts on his horn. Half a dozen of his men appeared, and surrounded the sheriff.

"I have eaten in your hall today, and paid for the privilege. And I have given my compliments to your lady, too. Now you shall return the honor," said Robin.

The outlaws escorted the sheriff, blindfolded, down the winding ways to their secret camp. When they took off the blindfold, he saw Robin, and Marian, with a merry laugh on her lips.

So the sheriff had to dine on venison poached from under his very nose, and wine stolen from his own cellars. And Robin made sure that he paid three hundred pounds for the privilege.

They set the sheriff on his horse and led him back to Nottingham, a poorer and a wiser man.

Palfreys
Noblemen traveled on well-bred, quick-paced horses called palfreys. Robin drove the butcher's horse-drawn cart.

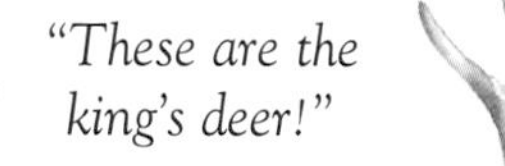

"These are the king's deer!"

Abbot
"Cowl" was the name of the abbot's hood, which hung down over his shoulders. Broad hats were worn by clergymen when outside or traveling.

Crusader
The Crusades were holy wars against the Muslims in the Middle East. There were eight Crusades between 1095 and 1270. King Richard was one of the leaders of the Third Crusade, which began in 1190 and ended in 1192.

Prisoner
On the way home from the Crusade, Richard was captured by Leopold of Austria and held prisoner in Dürnstein Castle, near Vienna.

Leopold of Austria

Chapter eight

THE RETURN OF THE KING

ONE AUTUMN DAY, Robin stopped an abbot, wearing a cowl and a broad hat, and a monk on the road through the forest. "Sir abbot," said Robin, "stay awhile with us. We are poor freemen of the forest. Our only wealth is the king's deer, while you have churches full of gold. Give us what you can, for charity."

"I have only forty pounds," said the abbot. "Here it is."

"Thank you," said Robin. "Twenty pounds I will divide among my men, and twenty you shall keep, for I wouldn't leave you penniless."

The abbot said, "I may not be rich, but I bear great news. I spent last night in the company of the king, in Nottingham. He is back from the Crusades. Long he lay in the prison of Leopold, Duke of Austria, but now he has returned to reclaim his throne."

"God bless His Majesty," said Robin. "Now, surely, England will be itself again, and these bloated sheriffs will be brought to book. You have brought great news! Come to our camp and toast the king – and taste the flesh of his deer."

Afterward, Robin set up a target for archery.

The abbot said, "That target is too far away. The best archers in the army couldn't hit it."

"But the archers of Robin Hood can," said Robin. "Any man whose arrow misses receives a blow on the head."

At first all the men found it easy, but one by one they missed. At last, only Robin was left. Just as he was about to shoot, a bird flew up and distracted him, and his arrow went wide. Little John, still rubbing his smarting ear, roared with laughter.

Robin went up to the abbot. "I am ready for your blow."

"I am a man of God," said the abbot. "I cannot hit you."

"I will allow you to do it," said Robin.

The abbot rolled up his sleeve to reveal a surprisingly well-muscled arm. His blow knocked Robin off his feet.

"That arm has done more than hold a prayer book," said Robin, and he looked the abbot intently in the face. Then Robin sank to his knees, and said, "Your Majesty, accept my service."

The abbot was King Richard, and the monk his minstrel, Blondel.

The king said, "I heard two things about you, Robin. The first was from the sheriff of Nottingham. He said you were a traitor and a villain. The second was from the people. They said you were generous and honest. The sheriff is a liar. Therefore, I pardon you for your crimes, and restore you to your title and lands. Is there anything more I can do for you?"

Marian stepped forward. "Your Majesty, I swore not to marry Robin until you came home. Will you give me in marriage to my true love? Friar Tuck can marry us."

"With all my heart," said the king.

So Robin and Marian were married in the greenwood, where they first gave each other their hearts. King Richard himself danced at their wedding, and the minstrel Blondel sang:

Underneath the greenwood tree,
I found the maid who is for me.

Minstrel
According to legend, King Richard's faithful minstrel Blondel found and freed him from Dürnstein.

"I pardon you for your crimes, and restore you to your title and lands."

Richard's Crusade

When Richard the Lionheart was king of England, it was thought that the most noble thing that a king could do was to go on a Crusade. A Crusade was a religious war, fought for Christianity against its enemies. Richard's chance to become a Crusader came when, in 1187, a Muslim army captured the holy city of Jerusalem from its Christian rulers. A Crusade was called to recapture it. Knights and nobles, common people and kings, leaped to join. Richard departed on his Crusade in 1190. He did not return until 1194, by which time England had had four long years of John's misrule.

King Richard at war

Richard's travels

Richard spent nearly a year on his outward journey, stopping to conquer Cyprus on the way. In June 1191, he finally reached "the Holy Land" (this included most of Israel and Lebanon). He left to go home in October 1192, but he was captured on the way and held prisoner for more than a year.

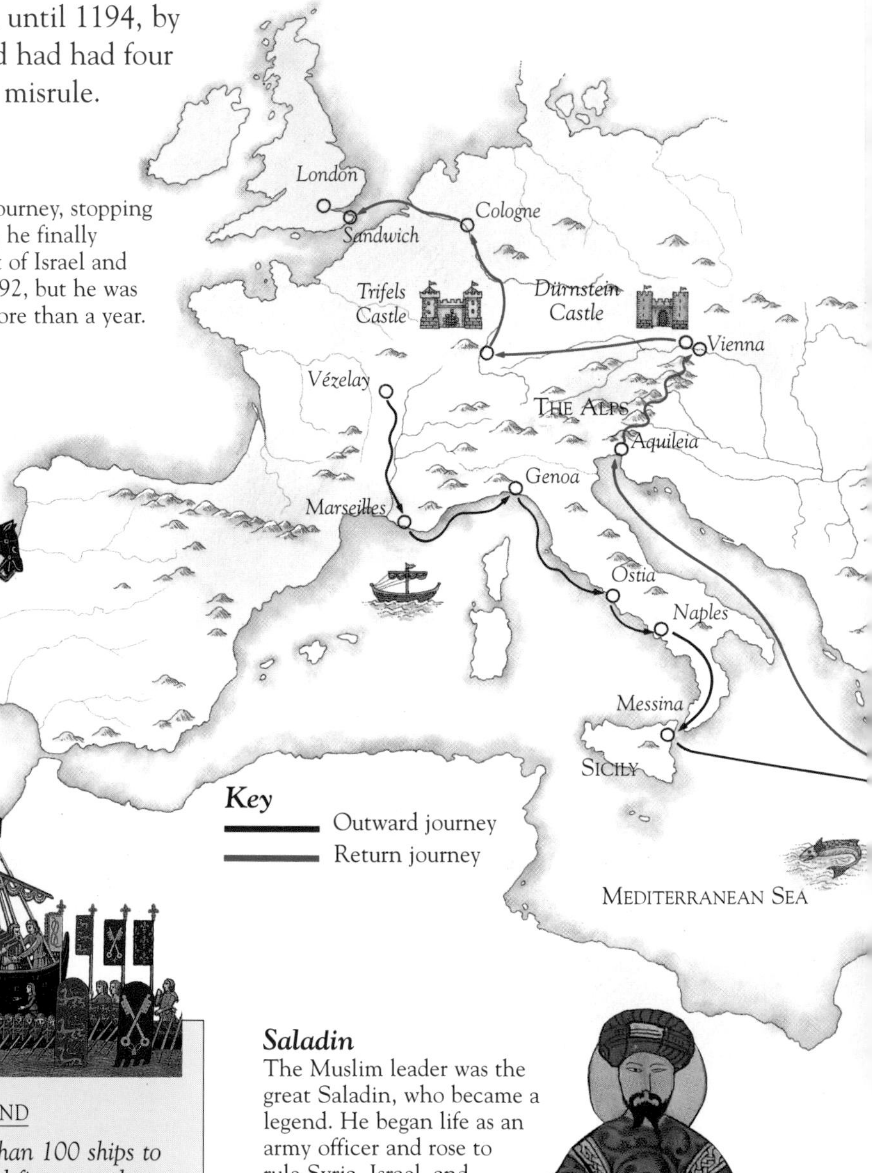

Monks bless Crusaders.

Blessing war

Normally the church was against war, but Crusaders were promised spiritual rewards. No other Christians were meant to harm them: Leopold of Austria was condemned for imprisoning Richard.

Key

Outward journey

Return journey

Sailing to the Holy Land

Richard assembled a huge fleet of more than 100 ships to take his army to the Holy Land. He had first vowed to become a Crusader in November 1187, but it took him several years to make his plans and try to make his kingdom secure in his absence. All his precautions were not enough to keep his brother, John, in line while he was away.

Saladin

The Muslim leader was the great Saladin, who became a legend. He began life as an army officer and rose to rule Syria, Israel, and Egypt. Even his enemies admired him as a brilliant and honorable leader.

The Return Journey

Storms stopped Richard from sailing home, so he had to travel by land. No matter which route he took, enemies barred his path. Traveling in disguise, he tried to reach safety. In 1192 he was captured by Duke Leopold of Austria just outside Vienna, and was thrown into prison. The Duke handed Richard over to his overlord, the German emperor.

Shipwrecked

On the way home, Richard defeated some pirates, then decided to travel with them. But they were soon shipwrecked.

Prince John and the King of France tried to make sure that Richard stayed in prison.

Soldiers capture Richard.

Homage

To gain his freedom, Richard had to pay a huge ransom and accept the emperor as overlord of the kingdom of England.

King Richard accepts the emperor as his overlord.

Way to safety

Richard had to cross the high, cold Alps, then travel through Austria, in order to reach lands ruled by his friends.

The king is captured

After being captured, Richard was imprisoned in Dürnstein Castle on the Danube River. Later he was held in Trifels Castle.

Dürnstein Castle

War in the Holy Land

Richard was the only Crusader commander who could match the great Saladin. He was able to capture the coastal cities of Acre, Jaffa, and Ascalon, and defeat Saladin in battle at Arsuf. But even Richard could not recapture Jerusalem.

A bitter struggle

War in the Holy Land was much harder for Europeans than war at home. It was difficult for them to maintain their supplies of food and water. Richard did not have the resources to take Jerusalem. In October 1192, he left the Holy Land, undefeated but without achieving his greatest goal. Saladin died the next year.

Richard's triumph

Richard's greatest victory was at the Battle of Arsuf, when he defeated Saladin, the first time Saladin had ever lost a battle.

Unfortunate city

After arriving in the Holy Land, Richard captured the key port of Acre. Its brave defenders had held out for nearly two years.

Saracen soldiers

The Europeans called their Muslim enemies Saracens. Saracen soldiers were fierce enemies. Their best troops were mounted archers who kept a rain of deadly arrows on the Crusaders.

The holy city

Richard's greatest sadness was being unable to retake Jerusalem, the holy city where Jesus Christ ended his life on earth. It is said that when he realized he could not conquer it, he refused even to look at Jerusalem.

The Lionheart dies
King Richard died in 1199. He was hit by a crossbow bolt while besieging the castle of Chalus in France.

Richard's grave in France

King John
John was crowned in May 1199. He has traditionally been thought of as a bad king. He promoted his friends to important government jobs and ruthlessly collected taxes and feudal dues. His policies led to widespread discontent.

Chapter nine

FIGHT TO THE DEATH

FOR FIVE YEARS, ROBIN AND MARIAN lived happily together, sometimes in Robin's old home, and sometimes in the greenwood, for many of the outlaws had continued to live in the forest under the protection of the king. But then came the sad news of King Richard's death. Prince John was now King John, Robin's enemies once more the power in the land, and Robin Hood an outlaw.

"I fear our happiness must come to an end," said Robin.

"Nothing could spoil our love," said Marian. "So I fear nothing."

Little John, who was staying with them, said, "If we do no wrong, no one will trouble us."

But Robin answered, "Last night I had a terrible dream. Two men set on me, tied me up, and beat me half to death, and took my bow from me. One of them was Sir Guy of Gisborne."

"What are dreams?" asked Marian. "Dreams are just like the wind. They may blow strong all night, but in the morning they are still."

"Nevertheless," said Robin, "I am troubled. Come, Little John, let us go into the forest and see what is to be seen."

Robin and Little John had not gone far when they saw a tall and strong fellow leaning against a tree. He was clad in a horse's hide, with the head and mane covering his face, and the tail hanging down behind. In the woods nearby, a woodweet was singing its mournful song.

"Perhaps I am still in my dream," said Robin.

"Stand there, master," said Little John. "I will go and ask this man his business."

"I have never stood back while my men put themselves at risk," said Robin. "Do not ask me to do so now. I will deal with this man, be he friend or foe. You go to the camp to warn Will Scarlet and the others that trouble may be coming."

So Little John set off for the camp, and Robin approached the man dressed in the horse's hide.

"Good morning, my good fellow," said the man.

"Good morning to you," said Robin. "I see you are carrying a longbow. Are you, then, an archer?"

"I have come hunting game," said the man.

"And what game is that?" asked Robin.

"The outlaw Robin Hood," replied the man. "But I am lost in this cursed forest, with its winding ways. I need a guide."

"I can guide you," said Robin. "No man knows the forest better than I. But first, as you are an archer, let us set up a target and shoot together, and see which is the better with his longbow."

So they cut a long, thin branch from a nearby shrub, and set it up as a target at the length of a strong bowshot. The stranger fired his arrow, but missed. Robin fired, and split the branch in two.

"That was a fine shot," said the stranger, "worthy even of Robin Hood himself. Tell me, stranger, what is your name?"

"I will tell you my name if you will tell me yours."

"My name is Sir Guy of Gisborne," said the man in the horse's hide.

"And my name is Robin Hood," the brave outlaw replied.

At once both men drew their swords, and battle began. The two deadly enemies cut and parried, dodged and thrust, their swords flickering in the sunlight as each tried to deliver a mortal wound to the other.

Mummer in disguise
Dancers wore animal disguises in traditional plays, called mumming. A horse's hide disguise symbolized courage and protection for the wearer.

Golden Oriole
This rare woodland bird, then known as the "woodweet," has a sad call of three fluting notes.

Sword fighting
Robin and Sir Guy wielded large, straight swords in wide cutting sweeps. There were few rules in sword combat. Combatants cut and thrust at each other until one was wounded. Swift deaths were rare; fighters usually died slowly from wounds.

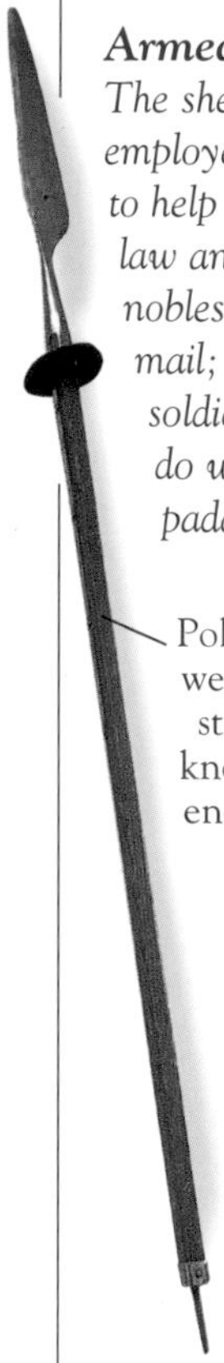

Armed men
The sheriff would have employed an armed guard to help him enforce law and order. Only nobles wore chain mail; ordinary soldiers made do with a padded jacket.

Pole-weapons were used for stabbing or knocking the enemy aside.

Meanwhile, Little John had not gone far when he saw a dreadful sight: two of his comrades lying dead on the forest floor, and Will Scarlet fleeing for his life, the sheriff of Nottingham at his heels with a party of armed men.

Little John drew his bow, nocked an arrow, took aim at the sheriff, and let fly. But the bow was made of young wood, and sent the shot awry. It found its mark in one of the sheriff's men, and sent him tumbling to the ground, but Little John had no chance to let fly again. Six men had seized him, and he was quickly tied to a tree.

The sheriff said, "John Little, you will be tied to two horses and dragged from here to a high hill, and there you shall hang on the gallows tree."

Sir Guy thrust his sword into Robin's left side.

"If that is the will of Christ," said Little John.

At that moment, a horn rang out – a harsh, discordant note that carried through the forest.

"Ah ha! That is Sir Guy of Gisborne's horn," said the sheriff. "He told me he would blow it when that traitor Robin Hood was finally dead."

The fight between Robin and Sir Guy had been a long and bitter struggle. At last, Robin tripped over a tree root and lost his balance. Sir Guy seized his chance. He thrust his sword, sending it into Robin's left side.

As Robin fell, he swung wildly. It was a clumsy stroke, but it caught Sir Guy unaware, and killed him instantly.

Robin stood up, blood welling from the grievous wound in his side. He took his knife and cut off Sir Guy's head, for Sir Guy was the only man who had ever shown Maid Marian disrespect. Then Robin took off his suit of Lincoln green, and put on Sir Guy's horse's hide. He took out Sir Guy's horn, and blew a rousing blast.

That was the noise that the sheriff heard. So when Robin arrived, dressed in the horse's hide, the sheriff shouted, "Welcome, Sir Guy, or, should I say, the Earl of Huntingdon."

"Call me Earl of Huntingdon," said Robin, "if you please." Seeing Little John tied to the tree, Robin took out his knife.

"Let me deal with this fellow, here and now."

"As you wish," said the sheriff.

Robin went up to Little John and quickly cut the rope with his knife, handing him Sir Guy's bow as he did so. He took up his own bow, and the two of them drew on the sheriff.

Robin threw back the horse's-head hood. "It is I, Robin. Sir Guy lies dead back there in the wood. I have cut off his head, and I will do the same to you if you do not leave this forest now."

The sheriff and his men turned tail and ran. Behind them, Robin fainted away in Little John's arms.

Cruel torture
Medieval punishment was as public as possible. Convicted criminals could be dragged by horses to their hanging as a warning and a spectacle.

Gallows tree
As an outlaw, Little John had no legal right to a trial. The sheriff could legally sentence him to hanging for killing his man.

Chivalrous treatment
Knights obeyed the code of chivalry, which demanded that they treat ladies with respect. Sir Guy insulted Marian, so Robin punishes him.

St. Mary's, Nottingham
St. Mary's was the main church in Nottingham, a church Robin knew well.

Confession
Most people went to church frequently to hear mass and confess their sins to a priest.

Box used for confession

Seals
The sheriff would have known a document was from the king if it had the king's seal, wax imprinted with the king's mark.

Document seals

Messenger
Kings, abbots, and nobles had messengers in their service who delivered letters and packages.

Chapter ten

IMPRISONED

THE NEXT MORNING, Robin went alone into Nottingham, weak from his wound, to the church of St. Mary's to confess his sins. All his life, Robin had been devoted to the Blessed Virgin, and it was in her church alone that he felt truly safe.

Marian begged him not to go, but he said, "I have trusted to Our Lady in worse situations than this."

As he kneeled down in church, a monk who was there saw him, his head bathed in a shaft of light from a window, and knew at once that it was Robin Hood. For the man had once been stopped by Robin and the outlaws, and had been forced to pay for his passage through the forest. He slipped out of the church and went straight to the sheriff with the news.

The sheriff marched on the church with a troop of men armed with swords and staves. When Robin saw them, he sighed,

"Little John, now I need you."

But Robin was alone.

He drew his sword, but was quickly overpowered and thrown into a damp, dark dungeon to await the hangman.

When the news reached the outlaws in the forest, some even fainted from the shock. They had thought Robin could never be outwitted or overcome. But Little John said, "Stand up straight, you weaklings. All is not lost."

The three outlaws who had always been closest to Robin – Little John, Will Scarlet, and Friar Tuck – set off for Nottingham to free Robin or die in the attempt.

On the way they met a monk, bearing a letter to the sheriff with the seal of King John.

"What is in that letter?" asked Friar Tuck.

"It is an order from the king that the sheriff must bring to him the outlaw they call Robin Hood," said the monk.

"I am as good a monk, and therefore as good a messenger as you," said Friar Tuck. The outlaws grabbed and bound the monk, and took the letter.

When they arrived at the sheriff's castle, Friar Tuck demanded admittance.

"I have an urgent letter from the king himself with his seal!"

The sheriff read the letter and said, "You can tell the king not to worry. I have the man in custody."

"I must see for myself, and then I will take the news to the king at once," said Friar Tuck.

"Very well," said the sheriff.

So Friar Tuck went down to the dungeons, and Little John and Will Scarlet followed. The jailer jangled his keys, searching for the one that opened Robin's cell. As soon as he had opened the door, the outlaws tied him up, freed Robin, and locked the jailer in the cell in his place.

It was morning before the sheriff discovered that the bird had flown.

Dungeons
Dungeons were normally in the castle cellars. The jailer was paid a fee to guard each prisoner.

Robin was thrown into a damp, dark dungeon to await the hangman.

Common songs
Tales of Robin Hood were originally ballads sung by minstrels to gatherings in rich households. Minstrels may have drawn on the ballads of ordinary people, sometimes accompanied by a pipe and drum.

Lily-flower
The ballad in the story, one of many songs about Robin's exploits, tells of his birth. A "painted bower" meant a colorful, painted bedroom. The "lily-flower" is often linked to death.

Witch
The witchlike old woman is like a "banshee," who, in Scottish belief, washes the clothes of the doomed at a ford.

Chapter eleven

THE FINAL ARROW

THE OUTLAWS FETCHED ROBIN away from the dungeon, but they made slow progress into the forest, for Robin was sick. His wound from his fight with Sir Guy was still open and raw, he had caught a fever, and his talk was rambling and confused. Robin could hardly stay on his feet. He stumbled over every tree root, and if Little John had not taken one arm, and Will Scarlet the other, he would have fallen.

When Little John called him Robin, Robin just said, "Many speak of Robin Hood, but never shot his bow." And he began to croon to himself one of the ballads the common folk had made up about him:

And many sing of grass, of grass,
And many sing of corn,
And many sing of Robin Hood
Know not where he was born.

It was not in the hall, the hall,
Nor in the painted bower,
But it was in the good greenwood
Among the lily-flower.

And after that he lapsed into semiconsciousness, mumbling and coughing, and sometimes crying out, "Marian! Marian!"

They came to a dark stream, and there they met an old woman in black, who was washing some clothes and wailing, "I curse you, Robin Hood!"

She was like some creature of doom from an old tale, and Robin began to shiver and shake.

"Are you going to bury me?" he asked.

"I do not like this," said Little John.

"Marian! Marian!" cried Robin.

"Where is Maid Marian?" asked Will Scarlet.

"She has gone to Kirklees Priory, for protection against the sheriff," said Little John.

"Then let us take Robin to Kirklees," said Friar Tuck. "The prioress is Robin's cousin. She will not let any harm come to him if he is left there to get better."

So the outlaws carried Robin to the priory and left him in the charge of the prioress and Maid Marian. When they had laid Robin in a bed, the prioress said to Marian,

"Leave him to me for now. He must be let blood, if he is to recover fully."

Marian laid her hand to Robin's forehead. He was feverish, and scarcely knew her.

"You are the light of my heart," she said. "Soon you will be well, and we will walk in the forest again."

And when Marian had gone out of the room, the prioress took her lancing knives and, opening a vein in his arm, let Robin's blood. But she did not close the wounds, for though she was Robin's cousin, she was in the pay of the sheriff, and she meant Robin no good at all. Her father and Robin's father had been twins. Robin's father, born just a few minutes sooner, inherited the title and lands of the Earl of Huntingdon, according to the law of the land. The younger twin got nothing, and had spent his life in bitter envy of his brother.

"By rights the title should have been mine," he would say. And he would make his daughter swear with him, "We'll get even with them one day!" That day had come.

Kirklees Priory
Kirklees was founded in honor of the Virgin Mary and St. James by Henry II (1154–1189), father of King Richard.

Bleeding plate
Blood-letting was a common medical treatment – people thought it rid the patient of "bad blood" causing disease.

Hospitals
Nuns vowed to serve the sick and set up hospitals to care for them. The prioress in the story is more concerned with worldly affairs.

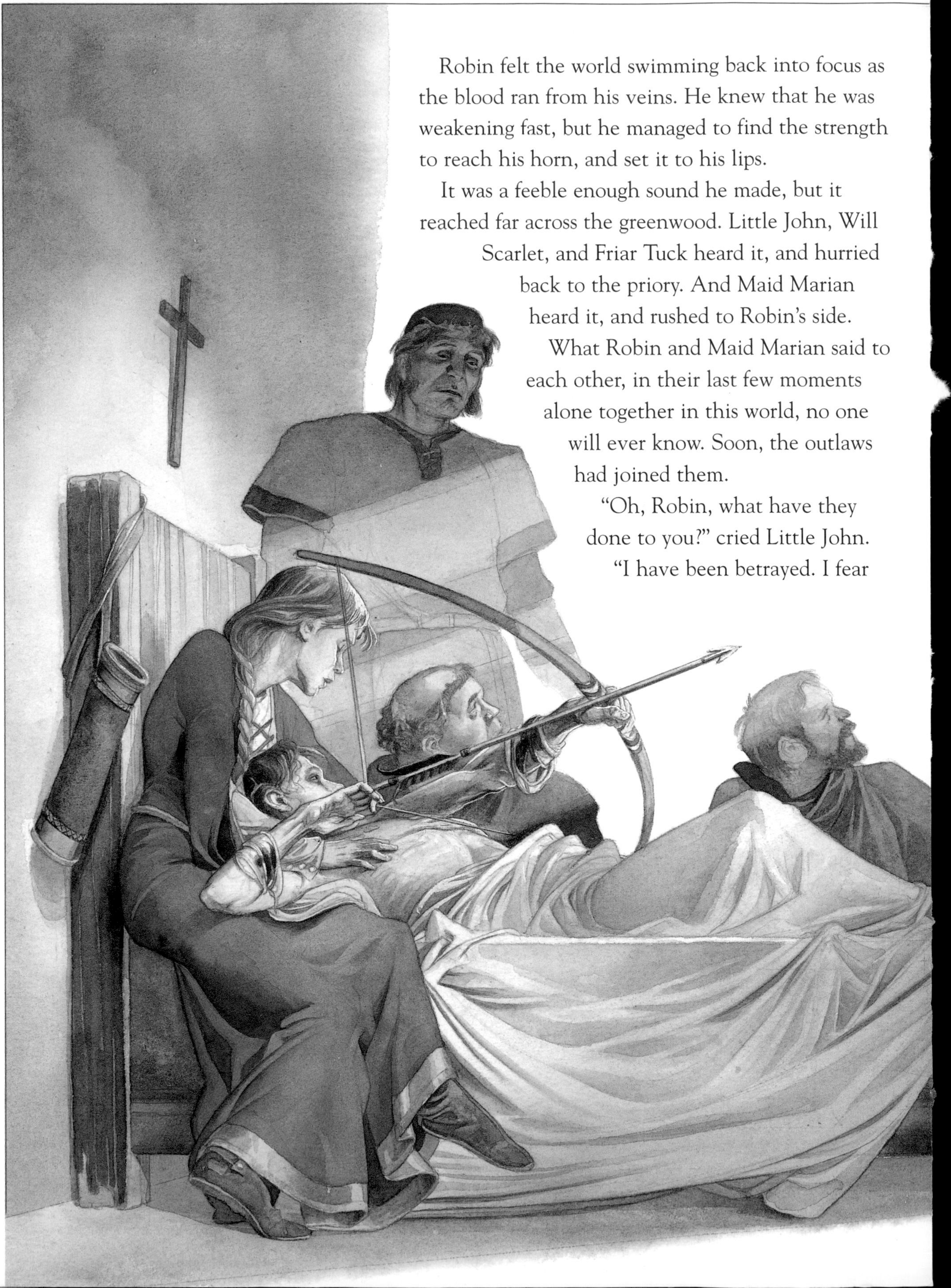

Robin felt the world swimming back into focus as the blood ran from his veins. He knew that he was weakening fast, but he managed to find the strength to reach his horn, and set it to his lips.

It was a feeble enough sound he made, but it reached far across the greenwood. Little John, Will Scarlet, and Friar Tuck heard it, and hurried back to the priory. And Maid Marian heard it, and rushed to Robin's side.

What Robin and Maid Marian said to each other, in their last few moments alone together in this world, no one will ever know. Soon, the outlaws had joined them.

"Oh, Robin, what have they done to you?" cried Little John.

"I have been betrayed. I fear

they have brought me to my death," said Robin.

"I will burn this nunnery to the ground," said Little John, his face red with fury.

But Robin replied, "Though a woman has murdered me, I will cause no hurt to a woman, even in death. Leave them alone, I beg of you."

He panted with the effort of speaking. Then Robin said:

"Bring me my bow."

With the last of his dying strength, Robin set an arrow to the bow, steadied it, and loosed it out of the open window. The outlaws could see its peacock feathers glistening in the sun, as it soared out into the forest.

"Wherever that arrow falls," said Robin, "there let me lie. I will be at peace in the greenwood, with the trees and the birds and the good red deer."

And with that he died, in Maid Marian's arms – the greatest outlaw, and the fairest man, that England has ever seen.

They buried him where his arrow fell, and set a stone there in his memory:

Here, underneath this little stone
Lies Robert, Earl of Huntingdon
No archer was as he so good
And people called him Robin Hood
Such outlaws as he and his men
Will England never see again

Robin's grave
Legend has it that a gravestone at Kirklees is Robin's. No epitaph can now be seen on the stone. The verse in the story was found in about 1700 among the papers of Thomas Gale, Dean of York.

THROUGH THE AGES

From the earliest ballads to the latest television series or feature film, Robin Hood has captured the hearts and imaginations of generation after generation. His legend has developed over seven centuries – the surname "Robinhood" appeared in records as early as 1261. Today, the stories of this popular hero still hold their power and are enjoyed by people all over the world.

People dancing around the maypole.

BALLADS AND THE LEGEND

The Robin Hood ballads were sung first by minstrels and later by ordinary people. The earliest to survive is Robin Hood and the Monk, *the story of Robin's capture. It dates from about 1450, and features Little John, Much the miller's son, and Will Scarlet.* A Gest of Robin Hood *dates from the early sixteenth century and tells the tale of Sir Richard. Robin also appeared in plays, and one of these, from about 1475, concerns Robin's fight with Sir Guy.*

Minstrels played instruments such as this gittern.

May games

By about 1600, Friar Tuck and Maid Marian were important figures in the traditional May games that marked the beginning of summer. As part of the games, men would dress as Robin and his band in order to gather money for the poor.

Maid Marian

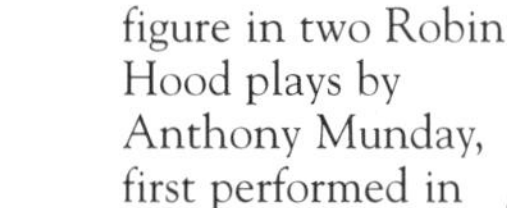

Maid Marian is a key figure in two Robin Hood plays by Anthony Munday, first performed in 1601, and in Thomas Love Peacock's 19th-century story, *Maid Marian*.

Robin in print

The anonymous Robin Hood ballads circulated widely in cheap collections known as "Garlands" – these ranged from broadsides (single sheets printed on one side only) to large anthologies. As the number of people who could read steadily increased, so more people learned about Robin.

Woodcut of Robin Hood, c.1600

A "Garland" of 1794

Morris dancers dressed as characters from Robin Hood stories

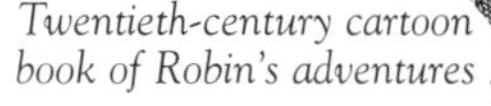

Twentieth-century cartoon book of Robin's adventures

Book illustration by Walter Crane, 1912

Always a hero

In this century Robin has been as popular as ever, both in the classic retellings of Howard Pyle and Henry Gilbert, and also in modern versions such as Geoffrey Trease's *Bows Against the Barons*.

Hollywood legend

Almost as soon as films began to be made, Robin Hood became a film star. He was just the kind of larger than life, swashbuckling hero that film-makers were looking for, and he is still the subject of massively successful films today. Perhaps the classic version was the 1938 film *The Adventures of Robin Hood*, in which Errol Flynn played Robin.

Early images

The first film version of the Robin Hood story was made in Britain in 1909, and the first US version followed in 1912. The 1922 *Robin Hood* (left) starred Douglas Fairbanks as Robin and Enid Bennett as Marian.

Errol Flynn as Robin, from a poster advertising the 1938 film

Here, Robin (Errol Flynn) fights Sir Guy of Gisborne (Basil Rathbone) in a dramatic moment from the 1938 film.

Kevin Costner became the new face of Robin Hood in the 1991 film Robin Hood: Prince of Thieves.

TOURIST ATTRACTION

Millions of tourists travel every year to see the sites in England associated with the Robin Hood legend. At Nottingham Castle, a Robin Hood pageant is held every year.

Bronze statue of Robin Hood in Nottingham

Acknowledgments

Picture Credits
The publisher would like to thank the following for their kind permission to reproduce their photographs:
t=top, b=bottom, a=above, c=center, l=left, r=right.

AKG Photo London: 10cra, 23cl, 23crb, 51tr, 51tcb, 59br, 62bc; Erich Lessing 52cl.
Ancient Art and Architecture: 11tc, 23br, 48bl; Ronald Sheridan 29tl, 50tl, 51cra, 62trb, 62cl.
Ardea: RJC Blewitt 23cra.
Bibliothèque Nationale, Paris: 25br, 28crb, 29cl.
Charles Best: 46cl
Graham Black: 8cr, 9bl, 13br, 14tl, 59tr, 61br, 62cra, 62bl, 62bl(insert), 62br, 62br(insert).
Bodleian Library, Oxford: 11tr, 28cl, 44bl.
Bridgeman Art Library, London: Biblioteca Estene, Modena 19br; Bibliothèque Nationale, Paris 10bc, 23tl, 29tc, 29br, 30tl, 33tr, 41cra, 51br, 55br; British Library, London 10tcb, 10crb, 11bl, 20bl, 21bc, 23c, 29trb, 30cl, 31cr, 31crb, 31br, 34tlb, 35crb, 38tl, 39br, 41cb, 42bl, 46tl, 50cl, 51tl, 52bl, 55tr, 58bl, 62c; British Museum, London 12bl; Giraudon 41bcr; Lambeth Palace Library, London 41c; Musée Condé, Chantilly 19tr, 23bc, 28clb, 28bl, 45tr; Private Collection 59tc; San Francesco, Upper Church, Assisi 27tr, 29tr.
British Library, London: 15tr, 25tl, 29tcb, 33cr, 36tl.
British Museum, London: front jacket c, back jacket tr, 11cr(insert), 20cl, 23cla, 32bl.
Jean-Loup Charmet, Paris: 48cl, 56bc.
Christie's Images: 7 whole page.
Bruce Coleman: Jose Luios Gonzalez Grande 53cr, Dr. Eckart Pott 22ca.
ET Archive: 28tl, 47tr, 52tl; Biblioteca Estene, Modena 58cr; Bodleian Library, Oxford 40bl; Victoria and Albert Museum, London 21tr.
Mary Evans Picture Library: 18tl, 18bl, 29tlb, 56tl.
Forest Life Picture Library: 23clb.
Fotomas Index: 40cb.
Ronald Grant Archive: Warner Bros. 45br, 63bl; 62tl, 63tc, 63cl, 63cr.
Sonia Halliday Photographs: 51bl, 53tr, Jane Taylor 51cb.
Robert Harding Picture Library: British Museum 49tr; Bernese Oberland 51cla; James Strachan 8tr; Andy Williams 25cl.
Image Bank: Andrea Pistolesi 56cl.
AF Kersting: 28tr.
Mansell Collection: 15bra, Bibliothèque Nationale, Paris 46bl.
Museum of London: back jacket br, 11bla, 23 cl(insert), 35br, 56clb, 15br.
National Trust Photographic Library: Oliver Benn 9tl; Mike Caldwell 44tl; Joe Cornish 9cl; Martin Dohrn 55cr; P Lacey 37tr; Rob Matheson 43tr; J Whitaker 28ca.
Natural History Museum: 22c, 40cl.
NHPA: Vicente Garcia Canseco 23ca; Manfred Danegger 23tr; Mike Lane 41br.
Peter Newark's Military Pictures: 50bl, 50br, 51crb.
Nottingham City Council: 63bc.
Nottingham County Council: 12cl, 13cr.
Nottinghamshire Leisure Services: 24tl.
Pitt Rivers Museum: 59tc(insert).
Royal Armouries: 41tc, 41cl.
Tony Stone Images: Amwell 41bl; Michael Busselle 8tr, 22bl.
Jane Thompson: 11tl.
Wallace Collection: 18c, 40tr.
Warwick Castle: 11cr, 54tl.
Weald and Downland Open Air Museum: 22cr, 26bl.
Jerry Young: 14bl.

Additional photography: Andy Crawford and Gary Ombler at the DK Photographic Studio; Alex Wilson.
Additional illustrations: Hayley Simmons; Sallie Alane Reason, David Ashby; Rodney Shackell; Roger Hutchins.

DK would particularly like to thank the following people:

Angels & Bermans, London; Bridgeman Art Library; Graham Black; ET Archive; Mary Evans Picture Library; David Pickering for editorial assistance; Victoria Hall for research assistance; Joanna Hartley; Barbara Holden, Rural History Centre, University of Reading; Nottinghamshire County Council; Tales of Robin Hood, Nottingham; Marion Dent for proofreading. Models: Claire Penny, Nicholas Turpin.